THE THIRD CURSE

by

CLAIRE LUANA
&
J. SUNDIN

forest Tales
Publishing and Photography

ISBN: 978-1-948947-21-3

Printed in the United States of America

Forest Tales Publishing
PO Box 84
Monroe, WA 98272
foresttalespublishing@gmail.com

This book is a work of fiction. Names, characters, places, and incidents are the product of the author's imagination or are used fictitiously. Any resemblance to actual events, locales, or persons, living or dead, is coincidental.

Cover design by Christian Bentulan
Interior design by Forest Tales Publishing

To the truth seekers and the road trip enthusiasts . . .

This swoony faerie tale is for you!

Glossary & Definitions

Adder Stone	(At-her stone) a stone from the Welsh *Mabinogion* that allows the beholder to see invisible magic. In Celtic beliefs at large, an adder stone (or magical snake egg) is created by the twining of serpent slime and saliva, especially on May Eve, so named after the European adder, and considered a highly esteemed talisman among Druids. But in reality, an adder stone is a naturally occurring glassy rock with a hole in it.
Afanc	(Ah-vank) a mythological lake/river monster of northwest Wales believed to have caused epic floods and held responsible for many small village deaths (also called an Addanc).
Aghanravel	(AH-gan-ra-vell) a fictional city in in the Glens of Antrim along Lough Neagh, province of Ulster, Northern Ireland. Home to the fictional Clann Allán.
Breton	(breh-tun) People from Brittany (a region in France) or who speak the Celtic language of Brittany (similar to Cornish).
Britannia	(breh-tan-knee-uh) A Roman province that incorporated all areas of the island of Britain south of Caledonia (what is mostly Scotland). This term is still used to this day.
Briton	(Bri-ten) the people who inhabited the island of Britain before the Anglo-Saxon invasion and who spoke Brittonic languages known today as Welsh, Cornish, and Breton. During the mid-

Briton (continued)	medieval period, they inhabited most of the west coastline of Britain, even up into parts of Scotland.
Caerleon	(Car-LEE-un) A city in Southern Wales. Known as the mighty Roman "City of the Legion" and where King Arthur is historically believed to have held court.
Clann / Clan	(Kl-an) A tribe of close-knit and/or interrelated people, spelled "clann" in Ireland and "clan" everywhere else.
Dál nAraidi	(Dahl-en-ah-ride-ee) a Cruithne kingdom, or possibly a confederation of Cruithne clanns in the medieval era, located in Northeastern Ireland around Lough Neagh.
Druid	(Drew-id) a person in ancient Celtic cultures who belonged to one of the highest-ranking professional classes. While some were religious leaders, many were also legal authorities, presided as judges, bards (aka lore keepers and historians), medical professionals, and political advisors. In neo-pagan circles, druids are considered nature magicians as well.
Fiann / Fianna	(FEE-an / FEE-an-uh) In Irish mythology, they were small war bands, typically semi-independent. In history, they were usually young warrior nobles / war bands who didn't own land of their own or hadn't yet come into their inheritance.
Fionnabhair	(FEE-oh-nuh-var) the Irish cognate of the Welsh name Gwenhwyfar or Gwenevere, meaning "white fay" or "white enchantress"
Fomorians (aka Fomhórach / Fomhóraigh)	(Foe-more-ee-ahn) They are known as the "people/tribes (children) of the goddess Domnu," a supernatural race and the enemies of the Túatha dé Danann, the first settlers of Ireland. Though many from both clanns intermarry. The Formorians are typically portrayed as orcish-like giants with water-monster features. Children born of Formorians and Túatha dé are

Fomorians	considered extremely beautiful.
Grail	(Gr-ALE) From the Old French "graal" which means crater, dish. Grail's were common serving dishes. The idea of a "cup" or "chalice" is from the 13th-14th century.
Gwen	(Gwin) Welsh for a young woman who is so profoundly beautiful, you'll die if you gaze upon her for too long. A sacred and holy form of beauty tied to being a sun or moon demi-goddess, or a goddess of light.
Gwenevere	(Gwin-iv-eer) the English spelling of Gwenhwyfar, Welsh name for "white fay" or "white enchantress"
In-Between	The shadow "foggy" world in Celtic mythology that lies between the mortal and Otherworld realms. The place of "mist."
Lough Insholin	(Lock Inch-uh-oh-lin) means "Lake of the O'Lynn Island," for the Ó Fhloinn family, or O'Lynn, who hailed originally from Londonderry, Ulster, and eventually took over most of Antrim.
Lough Neagh	(Lock Nay) A large lake in the province of Ulster, Northern Ireland.
Ogham	(Ome) the ancient 20-letter rune alphabet of Britain and Ireland, used primarily by druids. Also used as divination runes in neo-pagan magic.
Otherworld	(Uh-thur-werld) also known as Tír na nÓg in Irish mythology, it is the realm of the gods and the dead
Pendragon	(Pen-drah-gun) the title given to the King of Briton during and after Roman occupation through the medieval period, primarily held by a king in Wales. Also known as the Head Dragon.

Sídhe	(Shay) The faerie people of Irish mythology (Túatha dé Danann) who lived beneath the hills (gateway to the Otherworld).
The Morrígan	(More-ree-ghon) the Celtic goddess of war and fate, the Great Phantom (Fay) Queen, often interpreted as a triple sister goddess. Also known as the "Crow of Battle" or the "Carrion Crow" and can shapeshift into a crow. Some scholars believe Morgan la Fay / Morgana stemmed from The Morrígan.
Tintagel	(Tin-TAH-jell) City in North Cornwall, where Arthur was conceived.
Túatha dé Danann	(Too-ah day don-an) is translated as "people/tribes (children) of the goddess Danu" and were a supernatural race in Irish mythology who lived in the Otherworld, but who interacted with humans in the mortal realms. They are also known as the first settlers of Ireland. Often called "faeries" and "elves." Though Irish, the mythological figures appear throughout the Celtic/Gaelic world.
Twrch Trwyth	(Tork Troy-th) The Welsh re-telling of the mythological faerie boar of Ireland (Triath) as found in the Welsh romance prose *Culhwch and Olwen*, where King Arthur assists Cullwch in completing one of his impossible tasks by retrieving a magical razor and grooming kit from the bristles of a monstrous faerie boar for Olwen's father, a giant, who must shave his beard before his daughter's wedding.
Uí Tuírtri	(Oo-EE tour-tree) A clann of Northern Ireland, descending from one of the three Collas, primarily ruled by the O'Lynn chiefs.
Ulster	(Ohl-stir) Province in Northern Ireland

MORAY

ALBA

◇ Caer-Benic

Castellum Puellarum
CASTLE OF MAIDENS

STRATHCLYDE

⑦ Lough Isholin
⑥ Aghanravel
⑧

ULSTER

ISLE OF MAN

Dublin ◇

Irish Sea

IRELAND

NORTHUMBRIA

GWYNEDD
Brunanburh
Betws-y-Coed
Chester

Maesbury Marsh

⑤
① Talgarth
② ③ Caerleon
ARTHUR'S KEEP

MERCIA

EAST
ANGLIA

Swansea
④

Severn Sea

ESSEX

WESSEX

Tintagel

CORNWALL

King Arthur's
Britain

① BUEITT
② BRYCHEINIOG
③ GWENT
④ MORGANNWG

DYFED ⑤
ANTRIM ⑥
LONDONBERRY ⑦
LOUGH NEAGH ⑧

"...there is more to a king than a crown, and far more to a knight than a sword."

John Steinbeck

The Acts of King Arthur and His Noble Knights

Prologue

Morgana

Briny air ruffled the crow's feathers as a west-erly wind skipped across the fathomless blue sky. Below, war tents and craggy moors dotted the landscape. The male who smelled of bitter lust and greed was nearby. Even now, high above the human clamor, she could smell his heart's whispered prayers.

The crow swooped low, gliding past sweat- and dirt-covered males and females and smoke-clouded cook fires. There. The hide tent with the ornate wooden frame. A caw rumbled from the crow and a nearby murder darkened the clear sky. Black feathers rained down, falling upon the encampment like dark, silent omens. With mortal eyes now fastened above, the crow soared low to the ground and slipped into the power-hungry male's tent, landing on his throne of black thorns.

A sharp gasp caught the crow's attention and she hopped on her feet until she faced the back corner.

In the bed, crouched in a thin shift and surrounded by furs and blankets, lay a young woman with hair like tumbling autumn leaves and eyes the color of freshly-tilled earth.

Delighted, the crow cawed and the girl startled back, unable to move far. A metallic scent filled the air and the crow fluffed her feathers at the blissful fragrance. A drop of blood fell from the girl's knotted wrists, which now tugged hard on the short rope that was tied to the tent's center beam.

"Please . . ." the young woman rasped. "Do not harm me, I beg of ye. D-D-Donal threatened that . . . that ye would peck my eyes out, if I . . . I did not please him."

Shadows and the desperate prayers of vengeful men at war wrapped around the crow in spectral ribbons. Brittle leaves on the tent's earthen floor caught flight and swirled about in a macabre dance. The small, young woman bit back a shriek and curled into herself to become even smaller at the sight.

Morgana relished Aideen's fright, settling into O'Lynn's black throne as a heady sigh left her chest. Her claw-tipped fingers gripped the arms for show, her black feathered dress fanning over her legs and ruffling as though a thousand birds in flight. "Now, now . . ." Morgana cooed in a saccharin voice. "What would your brave warrior sister think of youhis moment?" She lifted from the throne gracefully and moved toward the witch's kin slowly, each step calculated. "Does she know you are a coward? That you sold your pathetic life to a ruthless man to buy your father a few more days on this goddess-forsaken land?"

Tears gathered in Aideen's soft brown eyes and Morgana tilted her head and blinked. "You poor lamb." Reaching the bed, she slid a sharp nail down the girl's cheek, across the throbbing pulse in her neck, down farther to where the young woman's thunderous heart told Morgana everything she needed to know. A hidden strength lay beneath the fearful overtures.

She bared her fangs and Aideen stilled, a catatonic animal attempting to hide her trembling adrenaline. "I will not peck out your eyes today, for I have use of you yet. But you have given me an idea. How to torment your dear sister."

She spun away from Aideen and sauntered back toward the throne, saying, "If only you could see your sister now, writhing naked in the arms of various men, laughing, flirting, indulging in sensual pleasures, while you quake at the thought of the single touch of your husband. So unfair."

Aideen pushed against her restraints and spat, "Fionnabhair would never abandon me or Father! Ye lie! Ye're a queen of lies!"

"Do I now?" A faint smile played at the corners of her mouth. "We shall see."

Just as the words left her lips, the tent's flaps opened and Donal O'Lynn marched in, halting midstride. His gaze raked over Morgana and she twisted sideways, allowing him a better view of her breasts and narrow hips. O'Lynn was weak, easy to manipulate. A soft female body was all it took to stir his blood into submissive obedience. Morgana tilted her gaze toward Aideen, a cruel smile curling her lips, before turning back toward O'Lynn.

"You wed the girl, I see," she began.

"Aye, two eves past." O'Lynn strode toward Morgana.

She licked her bottom lip at his approach and his eyes shuttered. "I have visited the port towns of Ulster and spoken to several ship makers."

"Oh?" Donal slowed before her, his eyes taking in her curves, the ones practically spilling out of her slitted bodice. "And what do ye want with ships? I married the younger Allán princess to punish her whore sister and seize the Allán lands as my own. Do ye plan to parade my bride across the sea now?"

Morgana hissed at the mentioned of the witch and O'Lynn's eyebrows shot up.

"Ye promised me power," he practically growled. "Ye promised me kingship. I followed yer directions and the only thing I have at my hip is this wee slip of a girl." He leaned in close to Morgana and whispered, "A man of power craves more to keep him warm at night than this." He flung his arm out in Aideen's direction and the small, young woman sucked in a sharp breath.

"A man of power also craves war." Morgana trailed her nail across his bottom lip, before leaning down and nibbling the soft flesh with the points of her fangs, until he yielded to her with a moan. Satisfied, she flicked her tongue out to soothe the pain, then whispered, "Why let a female knight gain you a kingdom with a stolen sword when you can conquer a high king and steal the crown for yourself."

Donal separated enough to trace the curves of her breasts with the tips of his fingers, his voice ragged with need as he murmured, "Why indeed?"

"You want me?" she purred.

"Ye know I do."

"Bring war to Briton and defeat Arthur Pendragon and . . ." His eyes lifted to meet hers, his chest rising and falling in an alluring rhythm. The panting tempo of a stupid man. She blinked slowly at him. "And I will fulfill your every fantasy."

"I would die happy in your arms, Morgana," he growled.

She smiled as the shadows and whispers returned, swirling about her body. "Of course, you would."

The crow cocked her head and stared at the delicate young woman on the bed.

A tiny smile of challenge crossed her dirt-smudged face. A hidden strength, indeed.

With a flap of her wings and a loud caw, the crow leaped into flight and left the hide tent to join her dark sisters in the sky.

Chapter One

Arthur

Arthur slumped into a chair before the fireplace in his chamber, toeing off his muddy boots. Seven moons and seven suns had passed since he lost Excalibur and then regained his sovereign-blessed sword again. Seven days since he had almost executed the woman he loved. Seven bloody awkward days.

Never had he been happier to see his fortress—to be blessedly alone. The sheer force of will needed to maintain a demeanor of regal aloofness on the ride back to Caerleon had been exhausting. He had wanted to rage and scream and weep at how close he came to losing everything—his kingdom, his kingship. Fionna. But he couldn't let his knights see—these men who were as close to him as brothers—how much nearly executing Fionna had shaken him. Because no matter how close they were, he was still their king and, therefore, he needed to stand apart. And they were competitors for Fionna's heart. Even now. He made his knights swear that Fionna would never come between them. But he could feel the rip and tear already. In his own heart.

Arthur nodded his thanks absentmindedly as a set of maids hurried in, carrying buckets of hot water to a big copper bathing basin. His mind was filled with Fionna. He was all sensation and torment when it came to her. The sweet ache of the night they had spent together, the sharp cut of her betrayal. The staggering relief as she stepped in to embrace him, to accept his forgiveness.

Was it a mistake to forgive her? His heart shouted a vehement, "No!" But his heart wasn't particularly trustworthy as of late.

Fionna had tried to corner him time and again, from the very first day of their ride back. To explain or thank him, he wasn't sure. He just knew he couldn't face her. Not yet. He felt unsettled and raw, and the sight of her—the sorrow in her silver eyes— seemed to tilt his world farther. He had avoided her, attending to his horse, the fire, his fingernails, anything in the immediate vicinity that wasn't Fionna. Eventually, Lancelot had taken her aside and spoken quietly to her. And though her lovely face had darkened, she took whatever advice Lancelot had offered, and blessedly let Arthur be.

Arthur closed his eyes as the splashing sound of water being poured into the tub soothed his tension. Now, if only he could leave her alone.

rthur lingered in his bath for far too long, until the water cooled to lukewarm and colored gray from the grit of his journey. He had asked the others, including Merlin, to gather in his study after bathing and filling their bellies with food.

His chest tightened, and then a ragged breath fluttered free.

"You can't avoid her forever," he muttered to himself. He had nursed his wounded heart and pride long enough. It was time to put the events of the past week behind him.

Time to be a king again.

Arthur was feeling more like his old self when he strode into his study. He wore a linen tunic in a rich burgundy shade, black breeches, and polished black leather boots. The gold oak leaf circlet rested on his head and Excalibur swung at his hip. The sword would never leave his side again. Not while he lived.

He was the last to arrive, from all appearances; the other knights were arrayed in various chairs around the room. Lancelot, in a blue tunic that set off the black of his hair and the sky-blue of his eyes; Percival, sitting behind Arthur's desk, his feet up with a book in his lap; Galahad, dwarfing one of the two armchairs by the fire, polishing a dagger. And Fionna, in the other armchair, her hands in her lap, her head tilted down in a look of contrition that fit her about as well as a jester's motley on a yuletide goose. Her white-blonde hair was now washed and rebraided. But rather than a dress that would set off her curves and softness—a dress like the one she had worn for the faerie ambassador's visit—she wore a simple tunic and breeches like a man. At least, dressing for practicality suited her. And helped him to see her as a fellow knight—not as a woman.

Merlin strode up to Arthur and clapped him on the shoulder, pulling Arthur from his rambling thoughts. "I sense that you've endured an eventful week," the druid said. The gold rings of his eyes flashed with magic and compassion.

"That would be the understatement of the century," Arthur murmured, forcing a laugh. "Good to see you, my friend."

"Likewise." Merlin's hands disappeared back into the pockets of his coarse, gray robes.

Arthur marched to the front of the room by the fireplace and turned, crossing his arms across his still too-tight chest. "Have the knights filled you in on our journey?" Arthur asked Merlin.

"Yes. Though I suspect I received the . . . abridged version."

Arthur nodded. "Good. All the details of our trip to find Lord Bronn are not important. There is only one focus we must concern ourselves with now. Finding the Grail and curing this unnatural curse that has befallen Caerleon."

"Lancelot said the land's curse affected the river?" Merlin asked. "Caerleon's waters are poisoned?"

"That's what we saw," Galahad volunteered. "Everything the river touched withered and died, whether flora or fauna."

"We haven't yet received reports of any human deaths," Merlin said. "But this poison will spread quickly, now that the curse has fully begun."

"I will send word to the villages, instructing them to test the water before drinking from their wells, streams, or river," Arthur said. "This sickness . . . it is unnatural. Reminded me of old tales of Fomorian magic."

Merlin narrowed his eyes. "Indeed. They have not emerged from the sea's abyss in decades."

"Not the same as permanently banished, druid," Lancelot tossed out.

"True. And if they have emerged, we have much to fear."

Arthur pressed his lips together. "We must find the Grail soon or there won't be anyone in Caerleon left to warn."

Merlin turned to Percival. "Tell me of this stone you found. You are certain of the runic message?"

Percival sat up, pulling his feet off the desk. The copper-haired lad looked older, more world-weary. Perhaps he felt the weight of their quest settled squarely upon his shoulders. "Aye, I'm certain. The stone revealed a riddle to me. *Across the wall and atop the rock hill, the blessed five shall drink their fill.*"

"And you've interpreted this to mean that Caer Benic is in the Kingdom of Alba, located near the Strathclyde city of Castellum Puellarum?" Merlin tilted his head, considering. "I concur."

"We must leave at once," Arthur said. "Caerleon grows sicker with each passing candle mark."

"Don't leave in undue haste," Merlin said. "Knowing the location of the Grail is not enough. There are powerful magics that protect the vessel of the old gods. You must be prepared to face each defensive measure."

Arthur grimaced, though he knew Merlin offered wise counsel. "Very well. Tell us. How can we prepare?"

Merlin paced across the room, his gaze sharpening as his pupils narrowed. "Legends speak of three sacred relics that will aid the seeker in finding the Grail. The key, the stone, and the sword."

A tiny smile tugged the corner of Galahad's lips. They all recognized the patterned cue of Merlin's bardic nature as a lore keeper. A story was about to unfold.

"The Otherworld," Merlin began, "is comprised of three realms. The spirit lands of the Mother Goddess, the Underworld, and the *In-Between*. These realms are woven into the fabric of Earth and are as natural to her lands as they are unnatural. Three realms with three ways to enter but only two ways to leave, three ways to see what human eye cannot but five ways to unsee, and three ways to defend your mortal soul from immortal blood but only one way to truly lose your soul."

"Faerie riddles," Lancelot practically moaned. "Druid, our patience runs thin."

"Impatience," he hissed, his pupil's growing narrower, "is a fool's temptress. She will only lead you to ruin and shame. The real object of your affection is worth every wait, wouldn't you agree, Faerie Prince?"

Lancelot clenched his jaw.

"Where was I? Oh yes. The Story of Three's.

Three sacred relics tied to the Grail, each object won with a test. One to prove what a man will sacrifice himself for. One to prove the true measure of strength. The last to prove whom he will serve."

"The key, the stone, and the sword," Percival murmured.

"The key to unlock the Otherworld," Merlin *finally* began to explain. "The stone to see invisible magic. And the sword to slay lies for truth."

"Do you know the location of any of these relics?" Arthur asked, his stomach churning in endless knots. He had to agree with Lancelot. Merlin's words set his mind spinning.

Merlin shook his head.

"So, we have *four* quests now, instead of one?" Lancelot asked, incredulous.

"Perhaps not," Merlin said. "I know of a woman who might be able to locate the key for you. She is a Bone Carver in Maesbury Marsh. If I were you, I would inquire with her first."

"And if she cannot help us?" Galahad asked. "What then?"

Arthur felt the air in his lungs grow hot as panic began to boil in his blood. "You must accompany us, Merlin. I will fall on my knees and beg of you, if I must. I can ill afford to fail this quest. My people do not deserve to suffer for my half-sister's thirst for war and death. You are best equipped to interpret any clues we may find. And to neutralize any hostile magic we encounter."

Merlin leveled his all-seeing gaze at Arthur as his lips pressed into a straight line. "I am sorry, Your

Majesty, but I cannot go."

"And if I demand it of you, as your king?"

"The standing stone spoke of the blessed five. Not the blessed six," Merlin countered, but Arthur understood the underlying message. Merlin was not his to command, for he belonged to the gods, not man.

Gritting his teeth, Arthur turned away, nearly flinching when Merlin continued. "And unless my counting skills have fled me, you are the blessed five. Isn't that right, Percival?"

"He speaks truth," Percival said with certainty. It was strange to see the lad without a jest on his lips. Unsettling.

"And if I might say," Merlin turned his keen gaze to Fionna, "your fifth knight is strangely quiet. Are you well, My Lady?"

Fionna had been sitting silently, staring into the fire for the duration of the meeting. At Merlin's address, she looked up. "I am well. I will go where my king commands, of course. I had nothing of import to add to yer comments, druid."

Merlin's eyebrows nearly met his hairline as he turned to Arthur.

Arthur shifted uncomfortably. He understood what Fionna was doing. Acting contrite to prove her loyalty in the face of her betrayal. But this pale, meek version of Fionna wouldn't do. No, this wouldn't do at all. It pained him to see her so—the fight snuffed out of her, the fire doused. The Fionna he knew was a force of nature—a shooting star of passion and power. He thought he would rather lose her again than keep this caged, dim copy of the woman he loved. A woman he had pushed away in his anger and grief. And in his fear. She knew the beating rhythm of his heart, knew him in ways unlike any woman before her. As a bastard-born prince—and now a king—he had guarded himself from intimacy . . . until her. Another rip tore through his chest, the bleeding gap growing deeper. Wider. Perhaps the water around Caerleon wasn't the only thing poisoned.

Arthur gave Merlin a little shake of his head, shoving down his troubled thoughts. Caerleon needed to be his priority. Not Fionna. After they found the Grail, he could deal with the mess his life had become. Not before. Arthur met the Merlin's inquisitive stare with a quick nod.

Chapter Two

Fionnabhair

I couldn't bring myself to meet Arthur's eyes. My gaze darted everywhere else—the floor, the fire, the nick in my leather belt—but I couldn't bear the look in his eyes. Arthur may have forgiven me, but he hadn't forgotten. He probably never would.

The weight of what I had done pulled at me like a stone dropped in a pool. True, I did have my reasons for stealing Excalibur—and good ones at that. But now I knew not what would become of my father, Brin, and my sister, Aideen, while held prisoner by our enemies, Clann Uí Tuírtri. Surely their chieftain, Donal O'Lynn, would realize soon how I had failed in my mission, if he didn't know already. What would he do to my family in his anger? The very thought of how they may suffer for my weakness, for my inability to finish the one task O'Lynn set before me as ransom for their lives, tormented my tattered heart.

Nor could I live with how my knights suffered for my duplicity. I knew they did, each one, even the aloof Lancelot, who seemed to relish in my betrayal with black satisfaction.

Perhaps the weight I felt wasn't my guilt. Perhaps I am the millstone, dragging down those I love into the dark abyss where even worse monsters dwell. I held in a ragged sigh and chanced a look around the room.

The knights were leaving Arthur's study, filing out one-by-one. Galahad and Percival each slipped me an encouraging smile, one I tried my best to return. I thought I could find my way back into the blessed good graces of those two. Arthur and Lancelot? . . . Another story.

My body ached, more so as I pushed myself up from the chair. Only Arthur and I now remained in his study. He had partially turned away from me and fidgeted with a book on a shelf to appear busy. Pain from my shoulder injury throbbed, a pain I could account for. The rest? It was like my body manifested the sorrow of my soul—my heart. I felt old and worn. He appeared similarly. Gone was the boyish smile and the summer light in his earthen gaze. Now, dark circles bruised the delicate skin beneath his eyes; his beautiful lips pulled tight into a thin line. Still, I wanted to reach out, to do something to bridge the chasm of our brokenness. Our wound screamed silent between us, a jagged sensation that rippled the air.

"Yer Majesty," I said, not yet ready to leave. There was so much I wanted to say to him. The unsaid words burned within me. But he didn't acknowledge my request for his attention, though the sudden rigidness of his posture suggested that he heard me. I drew in a shaky breath and blew it out slowly.

"That night—" I began and stopped. A knot in my throat tightened but I pushed forward. "That night meant something to me. Ye mean something to me—"

"I have been thinking on the matter of your honor price," Arthur said in reply, cutting me off. He twisted toward my direction and snapped shut the book in his hand.

I blinked in flushed surprise at the harshness of his rebuke, of his dismissal of my heartfelt confession. The memories of our reunion on the road to Brunanburh—of Arthur's hands running down my back in soothing lines, his strong arms circling my waist protectively, me sobbing into his chest—now seemed a distant dream. He placed a carefully built wall between us and meant to keep each stone intact. Well, if that was how he wished our relationship to be, then I suppose that was how we would have it.

"An honor price . . ." I hadn't been expecting this, though I should have offered one myself. An honor price was a sum paid to the kinsmen of an injured clannsman as recompense for the injury. Was there any price that would make right what I had done?

"Of course," I managed. "Whatever ye think is fair . . ."

"I think your assistance in locating the Blessed Grail is sufficient payment for breaking your oath," Arthur said. "I realize what you sacrifice by remaining here." His face was impassive, but there was sympathy in his grass-green eyes that twisted my heart anew. How very Arthur, to worry for me despite what I had done. This gave me hope. If he worried for me, if he understood what was at stake, perhaps he could find room for me in his heart once again. But even as the fevered hope surfaced, I dashed it. Things would never be as they once were. I needed to hold myself apart. For all our sakes.

My heart most of all.

"If ye think this price is sufficient," I said, "I will devote myself to helping ye find the Grail and heal Caerleon. Yer land and people don't deserve to suffer such a cruel fate." The poison I had seen seeping through the lifeblood of Caerleon, of all of Briton, chilled me. I knew faeries could be fickle vindictive creatures, but to force such suffering on innocents was unjust.

And I had to admit, a part of me was curious. Percival and Merlin both had named me as an integral player in the quest for the Grail. Why? I thought of when Merlin asked me about my mother, his strange gold-rimmed eyes blinking in the dark. Why had he seemed so certain there was something unusual about my heritage? Perhaps I would find answers on this journey.

"If you join our Grail quest," Arthur said, "your help will repay this honor price and more."

I wanted to swear to him that I would never hurt him again, but I knew this promise was one I couldn't keep. After all, I hadn't foreseen how the goddess would set our fates against each other last time. How could I be certain heartbreak wouldn't happen again?

"I hope there is never more to repay," I said softly.

Arthur gave me a terse nod. "On that we can agree."

I wanted to reach out to him, to run my hands through his hair, to feel the firmness of his muscles beneath my fingers. But I stilled my hands at my sides. I had lost such privileges.

"I was also thinking on your family's situation," Arthur continued. "It doesn't sit well with me that they might suffer while you aid me here in Caerleon."

The air burned in my lungs as I held my breath.

"With your permission, I would like to ransom your family."

A faint gasp escaped my knotted throat, too overcome by his kindness, his generosity. Arthur attempted to hide a blush by pretending to inspect the spine of the book in his hands. "Of course," I whispered with relief. "I would be most grateful for yer aid. But I fear nothing short of Excalibur would be payment enough."

Arthur's mouth set in a thin line once more. "Every man has his price," he murmured. "Even this O'Lynn. Besides, my motives are not entirely selfless. Perhaps my envoy can discover the identity of this friend of O'Lynn's who set us all down this wretched path."

"Yes, please, if ye can save my father and sister . . . I would be forever in your debt." I let out a hollow laugh. "Even more so than I already am."

"Very well." He flit his gaze my way for a single shuttered heartbeat, before pivoting toward the bookshelf once again. "I will send my man, and keep you apprised of his progress."

"Thank you," I said, sensing I was being dismissed. I suppose this was a better conversation than I could have hoped for, far better than I deserved. I would take it.

I wandered into the hall, my surroundings dissolving into the roiling tempest within me. When my thoughts resurfaced to the present, I found myself ambling through the fortress toward the stable to check on my mare, Zephyr. Another loved one I had wounded with my foolish flight. Galahad had promised to send for the farrier, but I feared what the doctor might find. What if her tendon was permanently damaged? If I lost Zephyr too . . . I shoved the thought away. No. That would be too cruel a hand for the goddess to deal me.

When I entered the stable, I found a wizened man in Zephyr's stall, a puff of white hair at his temples. He seemed to be mumbling to himself as he examined her, disappearing behind the stable door as he leaned down to examine the cannon of her leg.

I started as another head popped up in exchange, this one a mess of black curly hair. Lancelot. I must have said his name out loud because he turned to me, his expression darkening.

"How is she," I asked, pressing myself against the stall door, then reaching my hand out to stroke Zephyr's nose.

"A strain," the little man stood. Despite his small

stature and advanced age, he looked fit and strong. His rolled-up tunic sleeves revealed wiry forearms, his brown eyes clear and sharp. "She should stay off this leg for two weeks at least, no hard riding for a month. But she'll recover. She's strong."

I sagged against the stall in relief. "Thank ye."

The farrier pushed out through the door, brushing the hay and horse hair off his hands. He turned to Lancelot. "I'll send His Majesty my bill."

"You always do," Lancelot said with a laugh.

I watched as the little man strolled out of the stable before turning to Lancelot.

He gave Zephyr a pat, and she lipped his curly hair in response, nickering.

I narrowed my eyes. When had they become so friendly? "What are ye doing here?" I asked. My tone came out more accusatory than intended.

"I see no need to take your treachery out on the mare," Lancelot practically sneered. "She's a fine beast."

"I know," I said. "I raised her from a foal."

"Guess that's one thing you did right," Lancelot replied, shouldering past me.

I narrowed my eyes farther and marched after him, grabbing his arm and spinning him around. I might be contrite around the other knights, but Lancelot . . . Lancelot infuriated me. And it felt good to feel something other than guilt for a change.

"If we're going on this quest together, we better find a way to get along," I practically spat. "Ye've been cold from the start. So, tell me, Sir Lancelot, what in the bloody hell did I ever do to ye?"

Chapter Three

Lancelot

Fionna was a biting winter wind and the scorching summer sun when angry, a true sight to behold. But Lancelot knew this dark, all-consuming emotion intimately—he was a master of icy fury himself. He was angry at her, angry at Morgana, angry at himself, angry at the whole damn situation.

He took a step closer to her, leaned in, then grit between clenched teeth, "What did *you* ever do to *me*? Besides cheat your way into our knighthood, lie to us about your reasons here, steal my king and friend's most precious possession, and make the knights of Caerleon fawn all over you like lovesick idiots?" Lancelot threw out his hands. "It's so hard to pick just one!"

"I didn't cheat my way into the tournament." Fionna pointed her finger in his face.

He let out a harsh laugh. Of all her numerated wrongs, that's the one that bothered her?

"I just made sure I had a fair shot. And yes, I lied and took Excalibur, but ye dismissed me the moment my sex was revealed! Why?"

Lancelot looked at the timbered ceiling, a muscle in his jaw pulsing as he searched for any explanation but the truth. That Morgana had cursed him. That she had foretold how he would love a Gwenevere, and that their coupling would destroy Arthur and all of Caerleon. And that he was growing more and more certain that the white enchantress foretold was indeed Fionna.

"The truth, Lancelot," Fionna spat. The way she hurled his name, the way her Irish brogue danced across the syllables, full of passion and fire . . . it nearly undid him. She stood just inches from his rigid body, hands firmly planted on her slender hips, waiting. He tried not to look at her lips, not react to the warm breath pulsing on his skin. It was nearly impossible. Her silver eyes glittered like diamonds amongst the drab brown of the stable.

"Why do *you* deserve truth when you've told us nothing but lies?"

"I haven't lied," Fionna said, her voice thickening. "Not about the things that mattered."

Lancelot heaved a sigh and flyaway strands around her face fluttered. "Your presence changes everything. We were a brotherhood. Allies, friends, kin. Now? I don't know what we are. Perhaps we haven't come to blows yet, but it's only a matter of time." His gaze caressed the curve of her blushing cheeks, her flushed lips, and drank in how her breasts rose and fell in a furious rhythm, before he continued in clipped tones. "We're . . . *competitors*. Rivals. Arthur thinks a promise is enough to keep us from turning on each other, but he's naïve." Lancelot's eyes snapped to hers once more. "I *know* human nature. We're heading for a fall. It's inevitable."

"Rivals?" Fionna asked quietly.

"For your heart, Fionna," Lancelot derided, rolling his eyes. Fool woman would make him spell it out?

She reared back a few steps, as if struck.

"Ye said *we* . . ." she whispered, her lips trembling. "*We're* . . . competitors."

"Would you like a prize?" Lancelot nearly spat at her. "Congratulations. You're beautiful and I desire you, like the rest of my besotted brothers. Are you happy now?"

"No." Tears were gathering on her pale lashes.

Lancelot closed his eyes, steadying himself, trying to rein in the wild fury galloping through his veins. He took in a deep, shuddering breath. "I made a mistake with Morgana and it cost us all dearly. Me, Arthur—Caerleon is still paying for my weakness." His lids blinked open and his gaze captured hers. "When I look at you, I see another mistake waiting to happen. So, I must hold myself aside. Do you understand?"

Fionna's shoulders raised a notch higher. "I understand. But believe that I would never ruin what ye and the other knights have. I wouldn't allow ye to turn against each other."

Oh Fionna, Lancelot thought. *Don't you see that you already have?*

She continued, "I would leave before that happened."

He struggled to keep his voice even, calm. "Then why didn't you leave?!"

"I—I tried."

"You let yourself get caught."

"Let myself?" her brows furrowed. "Zephyr injured herself, and the boats in the harbor were cinders . . ."

He stepped toward her again, their bodies nearly touching. Wanting her to breathe in every spiteful word, he lowered his face toward hers, and darkly whispered, "You are one of the smartest and craftiest warriors I have ever met. Yet you chose to take Excalibur without a clear exit strategy, in strange territory, on a black night, when you were weak from an injury. Fionna," he breathed her name, bitter, pleading, "if you had wanted Excalibur, *really* wanted that damn sword, you would be in Ulster by now."

Her mouth opened and then slowly closed as she took in his meaning. The whole scenario was clear as day to him. She hadn't wanted to succeed in stealing Arthur's sword. She hadn't really wanted to leave.

"So, you see," he said, taking a few steps back, wanting her to feel the sudden cold of his distance. "You've chosen to stay, even if you don't truly know it yet. But that means there can be a happy ending for only one man. Once you choose, perhaps the tension between us will ease. Still, for the unchosen . . ." Watching Fionna with whoever won her heart would be torture.

Fionna twisted a braid in her hand, her eyes fixed

on the hay-strewn floor of the stable. "Why can't .
. ." she seemed to draw her courage around herself,
looking up. "Why can't I choose all of ye?"

Lancelot snorted. "That's a bit greedy of you,
isn't it?"

She set her jaw. "Is it such an outlandish desire?"

By the gods, she was serious! "Perhaps not among
the faerie folk, but humans generally seem to gravi-
tate toward one mate."

"Perhaps in Briton, but not always in Ireland,"
Fionna said. "There are women in my clann and other Dál nAraidi who have more than one husband."

Lancelot raised an eyebrow, temporarily lost for
words. The idea was intriguing. He had always enjoyed the company of both men and women, and
society's prudish insistence on traditional modes of
virtue and chastity had always annoyed him. But despite his modern proclivities, he had never considered
such an arrangement could be possible in Briton.

"I admit, I have not heard of such marital rela-
tions existing in other Gaelic lands."

"There are plenty of reasons to take more than
one husband. To increase warriors for one's clann,
for political alliances, to keep the gene pool varied.
Women are equal to the men in Ireland. If a man
wants multiple wives to bear him sons to farm and
daughters to gain him bride prices, then a woman
can have multiple husbands for a stronger homestead
and financial prestige among her clannsmen." Fionna softened her voice and said, "Least of all reasons?
That ye love yer men."

"And here, when I was with two women, I got

a whole kingdom cursed," Lancelot remarked dryly.

"I always thought Morgana's reaction too harsh . . ." Fionna shifted on her feet and cleared her throat, her gaze darting around the stables. "I am not suggesting such an arrangement between us. I don't even know if such a relationship would be possible here, or if the other men would desire or tolerate this solution. All I know is that I feel a tie between each of us, a kinship that I cannot deny. My heart belongs to each of ye. The sacred five Merlin speaks of? Perhaps we are more than our simple number of knights."

Lancelot nodded begrudgingly. He felt this connection too. There was something that tied them together. This tether had always existed. Though, he had previously thought those intimate feelings just the mere bonds of brotherhood, his affection and regard for the warriors whom he had grown up with and respected. But Fionna's addition had completed the circle somehow. No, not a circle. A pentacle. With each point inextricably linked to the other.

"Perhaps ye do not trust me yet," she continued in his silence. "But ye have my word, Lancelot. I will not tear yer brotherhood apart. Perhaps we can find a way . . . where no one needs to choose. And no one is left in the cold."

The silvered ice of her eyes bore into the glacial blue of his, challenging him to see the possibility. That each of them could find love in Fionna's arms, and she in theirs? A beautiful dream.

But only a dream. For no matter what happiness the other knights found. Morgana ensured that cold, aching loneliness would be the only future in store

Chapter Four

Percival

fo...m.

Percival was a fount of nervous energy as he bounded across the keep toward the stable yard. He could hardly believe this day was truly here. They were riding out to find the Blessed Grail. Years he had been waiting, learning, chaffing under the weight of his father's legacy, his Fisher King heritage. Yet now someone had smiled upon him. The Mother Goddess? The sídhe, perhaps? Who the hell really knew? Whoever they were, they had shown him something that could save Caerleon, save his king's rule.

Finally, Percival would have a chance to prove his worth to his king and his fellow knights. Not to mention relieve himself of this cursed vow of chastity. Good riddance there.

Their fifth knight was in Zephyr's stall, a wistful smile on her face as she brushed down her mare.

"Fionna!" Percival said, and then winced at how his greeting came out—far too eager and excited, like a little boy before a giant rain puddle. If he were to compete for Fionna's heart, she needed to see him as more than a green lad. He was a man. A warrior. A sídhe-blessed Grail prince. He cleared his throat, lowering his voice a touch. "How is she?" he asked.

"On the mend," Fionna said, giving Zephyr a final pat. "Feels wrong to journey without her, ye know?"

"She'll be fat and happy when we return, ye'll see." Percival smiled. "Do ye need a mount for the trek?"

"Already handled," Galahad boomed in his deep baritone, leading a saddled white mare from her stall.

Percival pursed his lips. Of course Galahad was already here, seeing to Fionna's every need. He was a worthy opponent for their lady knight's heart, and Percival's excitement over their departure dimmed.

"Aster is a fine mount," Percival murmured in quiet reassurance. Fionna quirked an eyebrow at his apparent shift in mood, so he quickly added, "Swift and surefooted. She'll treat ye well until ye get back to Zephyr."

"Thank ye both." A touch of a wry smile flitted across Fionna's face.

Percival pushed into Kit's stall, pulling his tack off the hooks on the wall. When he turned, he was surprised to find Fionna lingering there by the door, watching him work. She rested her elbows over the stall door, gnawing the inside of her bottom lip, her eyes darting around Kit's stall, looking everywhere but him. Uncertainty was an uncommon look on her, and he furrowed his brows.

"Percival," she said, hesitating. "I haven't had a chance to thank ye."

"Och, lass. Fer what?" he asked innocently, though he knew of what she spoke.

Fionna rolled her eyes. How did she make an eyeroll look so lovely? "Ye know what, ye wily fox. For riding to my rescue at the last moment. For vouching for me. For stopping Arthur from . . ." she swallowed.

"Nae, he wouldn't have," Percival said.

"He seemed fairly intent upon his course," Fionna countered.

"I helped remind him, sure. But Arthur would have stayed his hand, ye ken? It's not in his nature. He sees the truth in people, and judges them thusly. And ye, dove, are a good person."

"Am I, now?" she let out a harsh laugh, examining her fingernails. "I feel I hardly know myself anymore. Ever since I came to Caerleon, I've felt . . ."

"Confused? Overwhelmed?" Percival suggested, throwing his saddle over Kit's withers. He knew what she was experiencing. The first couple of months had been much the same for him when he had first come here. "Arthur is like . . . a lodestone. I don't know if the attraction is because of Excalibur, or this place, or the Pendragon lineage, but he pulls people to him— he shapes the course of their lives by his very presence. It's easier if ye dinnae resist."

A smile quirked on her lips. "When did ye become so wise?"

"Stick with me dove, I'm full of surprises." Percival winked at her.

Fionna laughed, the sound bright as a babbling brook yet soft like snowfall on leaves. It warmed him. She had been too quiet and withdrawn since they had returned from Ewloe.

"I almost feel normal with ye," Fionna said. "Though I know that's not possible."

Percival gave an experimental tug on Kit's girth. The gelding liked to hold his breath to keep Percival from buckling his saddle as tightly has he should. *Clever beast.* Percival pulled the strap another notch tighter. Then he pushed open the stall door, and Fionna backed up, holding the door open for him. "Ye can feel normal with me," Percival said, as Fionna fell into step beside him. "I know ye may not believe me for a time, lass. But I forgive ye."

"I'm grateful to have one of ye on my side," she said.

"They'll come around," Percival said. "We understand yer reasons. I might have stolen Excalibur myself, were I in yer position. Well, except for the part about kissing the daylights out of Arthur. He's not my type."

Fionna's face turned scarlet. "Ye know about . . . our night together?" she whispered.

"Our rooms shared a wall. I've heard Arthur snore, and the sounds coming from his room were certainly not the snoring kinds."

Fionna buried her face into her hands.

"Never fear, My Lady," Percival said cheerfully. "I consider ye kissing the king a mere setback in my plans to convince ye that I am the knight most deserving of yer affection."

His tone was lighthearted, to put her at ease and numb her embarrassment. But he meant every word. Fionna had neither declared that her heart belonged to Arthur nor Galahad, despite having shared intimate moments with each. That meant Percival still had a chance.

Fionna placed a hand on his shoulder and smiled. "Percival, ye wonderful, foolish man."

"We usually leave off the 'wonderful' part," Galahad said, swaggering over, looking as big and as brash as ever. Percival swallowed a moment of envy. It wasn't fair to have to compete with muscles like those. But, he reminded himself, what Galahad offered in brawn, Percival more than made up for in wit. And what woman didn't like to laugh?

Arthur and Lancelot were standing across the stable yard, speaking quietly, as servants affixed heavy saddlebags to their mounts, laden with provisions for the journey.

A look of quiet thunder crossed Arthur's face as he saw Fionna standing between Percival and Galahad. His hand strayed to Excalibur at his side, as if checking that the sword was still there. Percival stifled a sigh. He *did* believe that the easy peace they had once enjoyed between the five of them would return. But healing took time.

Arthur and Lancelot strode into the stables, their boots crunching over the dried meadow grasses strewn across the yard. Lancelot caught Percival's eye, a dark look on the man's handsome face as he darted quick look at Fionna before seeking Percival's attention once more. Percival cocked his head and arched an eyebrow, a gesture that seemed to calm their dark knight a smidgeon. A reaction that also made Percival's pulse secretly blush. For some odd reason, the man seemed to quietly seek Percival's comfort, and often. Lancelot answered Percival's silent questions with a faint shake of his head, before crossing muscular arms over his chest and returning his focus back on Arthur.

Percival studied the way Lancelot's soft black curls fell across the frosty blue of his eyes and how a light shadow of stubble covered the firm set of his jaw. A strange tingle brewed in his chest, one Percival didn't quite understand. Or had ever when around him.

Blinking back the direction of his thoughts, Percival offered Arthur a nod and asked, "Are we ready, My King?"

"As ready as we can be for a journey into the unknown." Arthur's voice was clear and strong. Percival recognized the tone—the one he used for kingly speeches and formal occasions. A tone that hardly seemed appropriate for just the five of them.

Percival opened his mouth to make a quip, but a black look from Lancelot shut it again. Percival narrowed his eyes playfully in reply, resisting the urge to stick his tongue out instead. Fine. If Arthur needed to hold himself apart, then so be it.

Arthur continued. "We all heard Merlin. We may face trials and tests, strange and foreign magics. The guardians of the Grail will not yield their sacred vessel willingly. First, we must find this relic, and then we must prove ourselves worthy."

Fionna paled, though her jaw was set with determination. She had faced trials aplenty the last few days. Percival didn't blame her for not wanting to forge ahead so soon.

"Should any of you encounter or feel anything strange, no matter how seemingly inconsequential, you share it. Especially you, Percival," Arthur said. "We can't afford to miss a clue. Or a warning."

The knights nodded.

"Then we ride to Castellum Puellarum," Arthur said. "To hunt a Grail."

"Your Majesty!" A servant in Arthur's red and gold livery was running from the direction of the keep, his round face red. He blew out a breath as he skittered to a stop before them, giving a hasty bow. "Your Majesty, a messenger."

"What is it?" Arthur asked, his eyebrows drawing together.

"There's been an attack near Talgarth," the man panted.

"What kind of an attack?"

"The Twrch Trwyth."

Arthur recoiled, and Lancelot let out a string of curses under his breath.

"The Twrch Trwyth in the Kingdom of Gwent?" Arthur's hand tightened on Excalibur's hilt.

"What is this . . ." Galahad stumbled over the name. "Twrch Trwyth?"

Fionna's lips thinned to a straight line. "A legendary faerie boar from Ireland."

"Though, this is not the first time Twrch Trwyth has visited Wales," Arthur added. To Galahad, he said, "I grew up on stories of this faerie boar. The monster was responsible for the destruction of many villages, leaving a path of ravaged homes, crops, and livestock across several neighboring kingdoms nearly a century ago."

"I thought the faerie boar was killed during Culhwch's impossible tasks?" Fionna asked.

Arthur considered her, as if forgetting that she was in their company. "I was under the same impression. I was told the faerie boar fell off a cliff into the sea."

Fionna's eyes widened. "To the realm of the Fomorians."

"This could be another of Morgana's schemes," Lancelot practically spat. "Designed to keep us from the Grail and, thus, the cure for her curse. The curse is the more pressing threat."

"Perhaps," Arthur said to Lancelot. "But the Twrch Trwyth rampaging through my lands will leave a trail of carnage behind even more quickly than the curse. Talgarth is on the way to Conwy, if we continue this path as you and I had discussed in the war room." Arthur turned to the servant. "Tell whoever brought these dark tidings that King Arthur and his knights will ride to their aid."

"So, we ride fer Talgarth," Percival said, offering Arthur an encouraging grin. "To hunt a faerie boar."

"And *then* to Castellum Puellarum to hunt the Grail," Galahad added.

"This quest is going to shit already," Lancelot muttered under his breath.

Chapter Five

Galahad

 alahad rode through the thick forest behind Fionna, watching closely as she swayed with her horse's easy rhythm. She held herself stiffly, as if even the gentle gait pained her.

"Fionna," he called out.

She turned to peer back at him, and a grimace of pain lined the set of her mouth.

Trotting up beside her, he asked, "How fares your wound?"

"Fine," she clipped.

"You're a horrible liar," he remarked. "I'm amazed you were able to keep your true goal from us for so long."

"The wound pains me still. There. Are ye happy?"

"No, not at all. I don't wish you pain. Did you have the chirurgeon look at your shoulder?"

"Aye, I did. He complimented yer stitching. There's nothing the wound needs but time."

Galahad frowned. "Arthur shouldn't have made us leave on this quest so soon."

Fionna let out a hollow laugh. "Yes, well, it isn't my place to tell him otherwise."

"I see what you're doing," Galahad quietly replied. "But by trying to appease him, to be agreeable and cooperative, is just another form of being false."

Fionna opened her mouth to protest, but he held up a hand. "This quest doesn't need your placating. Our mission, our very lives need your fire and your fight. Your wisdom."

"I don't know how to be around him," she admitted with a sigh. "I don't know how to be around any of ye."

"Just be who you are, Fionna. That's all we ever wanted."

"I fear I don't know myself anymore."

"You do." Galahad offered her a kind smile. "You didn't spend so many years on this earth without learning a thing or two about who you are. Just because a man holds your family for ransom—and forced your hand—doesn't change this truth."

Fionna nodded, but he could still see the uncertainty in her eyes.

"There's more . . ." Galahad cocked his head, studying her.

"Must ye all see so much?" Fionna said ruefully. "I never—" she started, faltered, and took a breath. "I never thought of myself as a woman who would marry. I watched as my friends and fellow warriors fell to love's fickle embrace, and I swore matrimony would never catch me."

"Why?" Galahad asked. "Why would you not want something so wonderful?"

"Is marriage wonderful? Does not love cause many more troubles than it cures? The husband with the wandering eye? The chieftain who desires someone else's bride? The young maiden who ends up pregnant and shunned by her tribe? Or shackled to some oaf who never wanted more than a roll in the hay?"

"Rather cynical," Galahad said. "Was there no one in your life who was happy in love? What about your parents?"

Fionna's silver eyes grew wistful, distant as the fog on the moor, and Galahad realized his misstep.

"My mother died when I was young. My father mourned her. He mourns her still."

"But he has you, and your sister. He never would have, if not for love."

Fionna snorted and gave him a playful push. "Must ye insist upon finding a positive angle for every one of my thoughts? Can a woman not wallow for a while in her own morose feelings?"

"Perhaps for a while," Galahad said with a wink. "But I'm afraid if you wallow much more, I'll have to unleash Percival on you. And he is far more annoyingly positive than I."

"Ye dare not." Fionna laughed.

"Oh, I dare." Galahad raised an eyebrow. The sight of her smile warmed him. Around her, his thoughts were peaceful, though he knew how her betrayal should trouble him. He couldn't bring himself to hate himself for enjoying the pleasure of her company, or worry for her loyalty. Perhaps Lancelot and Arthur doubted her but, somehow, he knew. He saw her soul—deep down where she hid herself—and she was as pure as a mountain stream, and as soft as the breath of a butterfly's wings.

"Galahad . . ." she said. "I kissed Arthur."

"Yes, the night of the faerie wine. Arthur told me."

"No." She shook her head. Her features were twisted, sorrowful. "The night I took Excalibur."

He stilled as details came into focus. Fionna kissed Arthur . . . and then took his sword? "Perhaps," Galahad began, slowly, "I now understand his upset more than I did before."

"Yer not angry with me? After what we . . . shared?"

He tested the feelings within him, like taking the temperature of water, or feeling for the direction of the wind. No, he didn't think he was angry at her. He could see that each of the knights meant something to Fionna, and her to them.

"Do you want me to be mad at you?" he asked softly.

"No," she admitted, squeezing her eyes shut. "If ye were angry with me . . ." her voice wavered. "I don't know how I could bear it."

"Peace Fionna." Galahad reached between them and rested a gentle hand on her thigh. Her leg was warm and firm, and the simple feel of her filled his veins with fire. "Thank you for telling me."

She seemed surprised, but looked down at his hand, and rested hers on top. Her fingers were gentle, tentative. They held none of the sureness of their games in his chamber. That woman seemed a distant memory. But he would find her again.

"Yer welcome," Fionna whispered.

"But don't think I don't know what you're doing."

"What am I doing?"

"Trying to prove yourself right. That love brings only pain. Don't involve me in those schemes. I'll have no part of them."

"I'm trying to tell ye the truth. There have been too many secrets between us. I never want it to be so again."

"Nor I, My Lady," Galahad said, and then twined his fingers briefly through hers, squeezing.

"There's a stream ahead," Arthur called out. "We'll stop to sup and to water the horses."

Fionna pulled her hand from Galahad's, perhaps a touch reluctantly, wrapping her fingers back around her reins. Her simple touch had buoyed him, filled him with light and energy.

But when they reached the river, Galahad's spirits sank.

Lancelot threw an arm over his face, burying his nose into his tunic.

The smells of rot and death were powerful.

"The curse," Percival said in dismay, running a hand through his copper hair. "The poison has traveled so far and so quickly."

Arthur's face hardened with fury. "We're less

than a day's ride from Caerleon. Another few days, and the sickness will reach the keep."

"Might there be any nearby rivers that are not yet compromised?" Galahad asked.

Arthur shrugged, the lines around his eyes deepening. "I can only hope. For without clean water . . ." he trailed off.

The knights looked at the brackish water, the bodies of fish and squirrels strewn along the bank. Summer was around the corner. There would be little rain in the coming months. Without these rivers . . . Galahad shook off the thought. They would find the Grail. They had a lead. The sídhe had smiled upon them and revealed the location to Percival. Surely, they must desire the curse to be broken as much as Arthur and the knights.

"We knew the urgency of this quest," Lancelot said. "This revelation changes nothing. We must continue."

Arthur nodded. "Indeed." And with that, he urged Llamrei forward into a gallop, plunging through the leafy underbrush.

They followed Arthur for a time, slowing to a canter. Fionna's jaw clenched as her shoulder jostled with each step of her horse. Galahad prayed that the wound wouldn't reopen on the trip.

Several candle marks passed as they rode in silence. Several candle marks since they passed Talgarth, the village still in shambles after the faerie boar. Galahad fixed his gaze on the horizon while the sun began to sit low in the sleepy sky. Around them, the shadows of trees lengthened to spindly fingers in the twilight.

"Shall we stop for the night?" Percival asked.

"We ride on," Arthur said. "The small village of Maesbury Marsh is close, if memory serves. There should be an inn we can stay at."

Galahad peered into the forest, his mind playing tricks in the low light. The thick bed of pine needles blanketing the loamy soil muffled the clop of their horses' hooves. A flash of movement to his right drew his gaze into the dark shadows there. He squinted, slowing his horse, peering through the crisscross of branches and leaves. Something shone white in the dark. Arcing like a bow.

His horse shied beneath him, catching scent of something and dancing away. Something dangerous and deadly. Stalking them. Galahad pulled his sword from its scabbard as the apparition pushed forward through the blackness, emerging into the dim twilight.

The beast was as big as a horse, with white matted fur, grayed with dirt and blood. A spine of protruding ridges arched across the monster's humped back. Black beady eyes gleamed with preternatural intelligence between two wickedly curved tusks as long as a man's forearm.

This animal was nothing mortal. It was nothing he had ever seen before.

And Galahad could have sworn he saw the beast smile before it charged him.

Chapter Six

Fionna

I heard Galahad's bellow first, his horse's panicked whinny second. And then . . . an inhuman squeal that raised my hackles like sharp nails dragging down my spine.

I spun Aster around and the mount danced beneath me, far too sluggish of a response for a war horse. A pang of longing for Zephyr lanced through me but was immediately forgotten when I glimpsed, in the distance, what barreled toward Galahad.

A beast of nightmares—huge and deadly.

"By the goddess," I breathed, my blood surging in my veins. "Arthur!" I called out, shouting to the other knights. I didn't know how far ahead they were, only that Galahad needed help, and soon I would too. I kicked Aster into a gallop. My mind went curiously blank as my honed battle training took over. With my sword in hand, Aster and I charged the huge white boar.

Aster shied from the unnatural beast as we passed, dancing and bucking beneath me. I struggled to hold her steady as I leaned out with my sword and slashed across the boar's broad backside.

The creature—it could only be Twrch Trwyth— let out a scream of pain as a line of blood welled along its ridged back. The faerie monster rounded on me with impossible speed, regarding me with feral intent—its new target. But a grim smile crept onto my face. For if the boar bled, it could die.

Twrch Trwyth charged.

Panic seized me at the sight—white flesh and coarse hair, dust and leaves kicked up into the air, tusks lowered to impale my mount. In all my training as a warrior, I had never fought anything like this. But instinct is a powerful force. Intuition possessed me within a wild heartbeat, and I dug my heels into Aster's flanks. She leaped away from the passing boar by a hair's breadth, huffing her displeasure. My braids blew about my face in the beast's wake. The monster's smell was overpowering—a musk of death and decay that made the bile rise in my throat.

"Over here!" Galahad hollered to the creature, who spun on cloven hooves, digging furrows into the black soil.

The thunderous sound of hoofbeats cut through the pounding pulse in my ears, and I allowed myself a split second to glance over my shoulder. A blur of three horses and riders bolted down the leaf-littered trail and I nearly sagged in relief.

Twrch Trwyth charged Galahad, and the knight spurred his mount out of the way, just inches from the boar's wicked tusks.

Arthur galloped past me like a man possessed, his face set and furious. Clearly my king had tired of curses and was ready to fight something flesh and blood. Something that could be killed. He stabbed his sword into the Twrch Trwyth's flank, burying his sword to the hilt. With a roar, the boar twisted away. Excalibur yanked out of Arthur's hands with the beast's jerky movements. Then the faerie monster rammed into Llamrei with its burly shoulder.

Horror welled in me as Llamrei reared and toppled sideways, taking Arthur down with her.

The boar's eyes went wild as the creature spotted its prey laying vulnerable and prone.

Large muscles bunched as the beast prepared to charge Llamrei and Arthur, who was struggling to pull himself out from beneath his horse. They would be gutted, for sure. I gauged the distance even as I spurred Aster into action, but I knew I would be too late. Arthur was too far away.

An arrow with white and black fletching zipped past me and buried itself—quivering and deep—into the eye of Twrch Trwyth.

The creature roared with pain, shaking its massive tusks while pawing at its face.

I whirled to see Percival on Kit, pulling another arrow from the quiver that hung behind his saddle. But I had no time to marvel at his incredible shot.

Twrch Trwyth was frantic with anger and pain. Terrified, Llamrei clamored to her feet, gaining the boar's attention. Arthur managed to remount, his eyes on the skittish mare beneath him and not their enemy. The boar noticed too. With a monstrous grunt, it ran at Arthur anew.

"Arthur!" I cried out in warning.

His head shot up just as Lancelot and his horse barreled into the boar's side, toppling the huge creature off its feet. Dust exploded in a yellow cloud as the boar crashed to the ground in a rippling heap of muscle and vengeance.

Lancelot angled off his saddle, his charger holding steady. Then, he pulled Excalibur from the creature's side. A stream of black blood cascaded over the faerie creature's dirty white flank.

Cheval—Lancelot's horse—danced back a few steps. Still, Lancelot spun in his stirrups and tossed the sword to Arthur, who nimbly caught the blade sailing through the air.

Twrch Trwyth stumbled to its feet, rounding warily on the five of us, seeming to reevaluate its prey. The beast looked even more hideous with an arrow protruding from its eye, black blood dripping down its snout. Hot breath panted from the boar's maw as the monster tossed its head to taunt us with those wicked tusks.

"We tire the beast," Arthur said, his chest heaving. His crown had fallen to the ground somewhere, but he seemed unconcerned as he surveyed their enemy with cold calculation. "No taking risks or playing heroic. Percival, keep the arrows coming. We bleed it; we all leave here today."

Another arrow whizzed through the air. The pointed head disappeared into the side of the beast's neck with a sickening *thwump*. The boar released a guttural squeal and charged.

At me.

Arthur's calm words rang in my head. I held Aster steady as the beast came for us, my sword slick with sweat in my hand. Then I dug in my heels. Aster sidestepped as the boar passed by, giving me an opening for another blow.

Or, at least, that was my idea. The boar pivoted at the last moment, moving with us—smarter and faster than I imagined from a mere beast.

Aster let out a wild whinny of pain as the boar's tusks tore into her side. The world tilted as the force of Twrch Trwyth's blow threw us both to the ground. My sword whirled through the air from the impact, and away from me. Then pain flamed across my upper body as I hit the ground hard with my wounded shoulder, stealing the breath from my lungs. The boar's screams of triumph mingled with Aster's shrill cries of pain and terror, creating a cacophony of animal sounds.

I drew breath into my lungs and scrambled from beneath her. Blood covered Aster's white coat, dripping to the decaying leaves below. I wanted to vomit. I staggered back on unsteady feet as the boar rooted and dug into her flesh and bone with bestial cruelty.

My sword. I lunged for my sword and then jumped to my feet as Galahad rode up behind Twrch Trwyth and stabbed his blade deep into its spine.

The creature screamed in agony. The crimson-stained head whipped up from poor Aster's exposed belly, spraying droplets of blood across me.

From the ground, Twrch Trwyth was huge.

Taller than me. I could feel the heat of its unnatural magic from here. My stomach twisted painfully, and my mouth parched as dry as a rainless summer.

Galahad had scored a good shot. The creature moved sluggishly now. A hind leg wobbled with a meaty step. But even the death throes of a creature such as this could be deadly; warnings rang in my mind as the boar fixed its one-eyed stare upon me.

I held my sword angled before my body, and the scene seemed to slow. My eyes narrowed at the foul monster. The beast who had just horribly maimed an innocent creature. This thing, this faerie monster, didn't belong on this earth. And I would be the one to send it back to whatever abyss it crawled out from. A strategy crystalized in my mind, and calm lapped at my pulse. Twrch Trwyth would charge me, and I would roll, before coming up and stabbing the boar's throat or stomach. Or both. It wouldn't survive another blow to its vital underbelly.

The beast leaped over Aster's prone body and came at me, but I was ready. I tensed my legs, primed to move when the mass of muscle and death drew close enough.

But another body barreled into me from the side, shoving me out of the way. A blur of black hair and brown leather and strong arms.

"Lancelot!" I cried out. The fool man had pushed me out of the way. And now stood directly in the path of Twrch Trwyth.

The boar hit Lancelot with an audible crash, tossing his body across the clearing like a rag doll. Lancelot hit the ground and rolled to a stop against a tree trunk, his arms and legs splayed like a dead man's.

Oh goddess . . . a gut-wrenching scream clawed viciously at my throat. My mind rebelled against the reality before me. Lancelot . . .

But there was no time for grief's heart-stabbing pain, only reaction. The boar was rounding on me again. And where I had felt calm certainty before, I was now frozen with fear and desperation. Lancelot had to be all right. He had to be alive.

The boar pawed the ground, appearing to delight in the scent of my fear. It was all the time Arthur needed. Seemingly out of nowhere, my king appeared on his black steed. A warrior's cry left his mouth right as he plunged his shining sword between the beast's shoulder blades, severing the spine.

The blow was instantaneous. Twrch Trwyth gave a weak mewling cry and stumbled to its knees before landing in the dirt with a teeth-rattling crash.

Eerie silence hung in the forest around us. Twrch Trwyth was dead. And goddess help me, Lancelot might be too.

Chapter Seven

Arthur

Arthur's heart hammered in his throat. Lancelot was tough. But to survive a blow like that? His thoughts stuttered and stopped.

Behind him, Galahad and Percival launched off their horses. Then all three knights—running and scrambling—converged on Lancelot in a blur of action.

Fionna's pale hands fluttered by his head, feeling for his pulse. A breath.

Lancelot quietly groaned. Stars above, he was alive!

Arthur released a ragged sigh, pushing back his surfacing emotions. He couldn't lose Lancelot. He needed his dearest friend, far more than Lancelot probably realized. While Arthur had his other knights, Lancelot was his foster brother—truly the only real family Arthur had left. His half-sisters made their position clear, their familial titles more tradition than truth.

"Give the man some room," Galahad said, pulling Arthur from his thoughts. But no one moved. They all needed to see. They needed to watch as Galahad probed Lancelot's chest, his abdomen, felt upon his arms and legs for breaks or rends in the flesh.

Lancelot's eyes fluttered open, his head tilting toward Fionna.

Galahad sat back on his heels, brushing a lock of blond hair from his eyes. "You have Hel's own luck, brother. I can't find a single scratch on you."

Lancelot reached out a hand and Arthur grasped it, pulling Lancelot to a seat. Another groan escaped Lancelot's lips as one of his hands flew to his back, his mouth tightening in pain.

Galahad was there in a moment, probing with strong fingers. "Can you move your legs?"

"I'm moving them right now," Lancelot griped.

It was true. His booted feet were stirring.

"Nice to see the fall didn't injure your sunny disposition." Galahad smirked.

"Ye fool man," Fionna said. "I had the faerie boar."

"You're welcome," Lancelot muttered, and then slowly, with Arthur's help, he climbed to his feet, his back hunched.

Arthur wrapped Lancelot's arm around his shoulders, holding his weight, and helped him walk.

After hobbling over to his horse, Lancelot sagged against the saddle, beads of sweat breaking out on his pale face. "I'm not sure I can mount," he admitted.

But luckily, the horses of Caerleon were well trained animals. Arthur tapped behind Cheval's knee, signaling for the stallion to kneel.

Galahad and Percival came around the other side and, between the three of them, they maneuvered Lancelot onto the horse.

Fionna stood back, her face a painted mask of anger and worry.

A crow's shrill caw broke through the silence, startling Arthur. He looked up and spotted a large black bird sitting atop Twrch Trwyth's corpse, regarding them with a beady eye.

A shiver ran up Arthur's spine as he studied the crow. There was something about it—the body was too big, the eye too sharp. The bird's caw too much like mocking laughter.

"A carrion crow has already arrived," Galahad mumbled. "Strange. The beast's foul blood is still warm. Are animals growing *that* hungry?"

"Make for Maesbury Marsh," Arthur said, ignoring Galahad. "Find the nearest inn. I'll meet you there."

"Meet us—" Fionna wrinkled her smooth brow. "Why won't ye come with us?"

"Someone needs to retrieve the tusks." Arthur nodded to the body of the great boar. "Merlin gave us directions to a bone carver. Well, now we have a bone to carve."

"Ye shouldn't stay alone," Fionna protested, hesitating. The others had already mounted and were now waiting at the edge of a copse. "Twrch Trwyth should have traveled south to Caerleon, not north of Talgarth. The faerie monster knew where to find us."

"I'll not be far behind," Arthur said. "See to Lancelot's comfort. Ride with him, and make sure he doesn't fall off. He doesn't look too stable." A stab of jealousy shot through Arthur at the thought of Fionna doting on Lancelot, soothing his hurt and comforting him. He shoved the feelings down viciously. His friend had nearly died. Was Arthur truly so petty to begrudge him a tender hand or a kind word?

Fionna nodded, uncertain, but followed his command. "Don't tarry long, My King," she said, looking back at the great white body and the black bird perched atop the muscular flesh. Then, she crossed over to Lancelot—who sagged forward while astride his horse—and pulled herself up behind him, reaching around his slumped frame to take the reins.

Arthur turned to the task at hand as they left. The boar. And the crow.

He picked up a rock, testing the weight in his hand. And then he hurled the stone right at the bird.

The crow launched into the air with a raucous laugh as the rock sailed by without a hit.

"Get out of here!" he shouted, picking up another rock and throwing it.

The crow flapped its wings, hopping off the corpse and onto the ground.

Arthur leaned over to retrieve another rock and faltered as the sound of hushed whispers reached his ears. The air around him grew cold for a moment and he straightened, his hand on Excalibur. There was magic afoot.

Dark shadows swirled around the crow, stirring the leaves and pine needles beneath its black talons.

And then those talons became black boots, feathers became fabric—and the swirl of magic became Morgana. In the flesh. Standing before him.

She wasn't natural—his half-sister. Her face too wan, her movements too sinuous, her form too sleek and curved to be human. She wore a black dress slashed with deep violet, and her black hair hung over one shoulder in loose curls. How Lancelot had ever felt safe to court this faerie, he knew not. She was desirable, that was plain for any man to see. But she was also *terrifying*.

"Brother," she said, a secret smile on her face. "Did you have to kill my pet?" She leaned down and dipped one delicate finger into the cooling blood on Twrch Trwyth's coat, before drawing a black line from her collarbone to down between her breasts.

Arthur kept his eyes fixed on her face. If she was here to unnerve him, he wouldn't give her the satisfaction. "I'm afraid your *pet*"—he spit the word—"escaped from its yard and strayed into my lands."

Morgana sulked, looking at the boar. "You were always far too serious. Do you never have fun?"

"None of this is fun, Morgana," Arthur grit slowly, his jaw clenched as anger surged within him. "People's lives are at stake."

"Human lives."

"Yes, human lives." He opened his hands before her, pleading. "Sister, what Lancelot did to you was unforgivable. But don't punish the people of Caerleon. You punished me. You played your jest on me by locking Excalibur in its sheath. You cursed Caerleon, poisoning her waters. Now you send this faerie boar? *Enough*, Morgana. Your grief is acknowledged. Two curses is enough." He hadn't been able to speak to her since the night of Lancelot's betrayal. Perhaps she had calmed down. Perhaps he could reason with her . . . get her to remove the curse—

"Two curses?" She threw her head back and laughed, her shriek sounding eerily like the crow's caw.

Arthur frowned, his hand straying back toward Excalibur. Was she mad?

"Two curses." Her lips curled in a wicked grin as she sauntered toward him, every sway of her hips calculated. "My poor foolish brother. You don't even know about the third curse, do you?" Her violet-hued eyes flashed with humor.

Arthur froze. "Do not mock me. What is this third curse of which you speak?"

"King of Caerleon, overking of Gwent, the Pendragon of Briton." She cocked her head, as if a bird angling to better see their prey. "So many titles, yet still you cannot inspire the loyalty of even those closest to you."

"You lie." Though, her words stung like salt in a wound.

"Do I?" She traced a fingernail down the drying line of boar's blood on her chest. "I do not think so. Whether kings or paupers, mortals are squabbling idiots. They are not fit to rule."

Morgana leaned over in a graceful arc and picked up an object from the dirt of the forest floor that glinted in the low light of dusk.

His crown.

He swallowed, stilling his hand at his side, refusing to touch his brow like he wanted.

"You and your treacherous father may have fooled Vivien, but the faeries of Tintagel see the truth of you, Arthur Pendragon. You are weak. You are failing. And soon enough, you will be *nothing*." She tossed the crown at his feet with a contemptuous motion. And then the whispers and dark enveloped her, and she was a crow once again.

The great bird cawed in delight, swooping toward him.

Arthur threw an arm up and ducked as Morgana's crow dove where his head had just been, before winging toward the dipping sun in the darkening sky.

He took in a deep shuddering breath as he watched her disappear, the ebony of her form melding into the black shadows of the forest.

Arthur leaned over slowly and picked up his crown, turning the gold circlet in his hands. A clod of dirt was caught between two prongs. He brushed it off and buffed it on his tunic. There.

He placed Gwent's crown back onto his head with shaking hands before pulling Excalibur from its sheath. He turned to the boar and began cutting, trying with all his power not to think upon the words now echoing in his mind.

A third curse.

Chapter Eight

Lancelot

Lancelot wanted to weep with relief when the first lantern light of Talgarth came into view. Every swaying step of Cheval's walk was torture. Shooting pain seared up his spine and down into his legs.

He hadn't been thinking. When he had seen Fionna standing there, so small compared to the might of the boar . . . his mind had fled completely. He would have done anything in that moment to keep her from harm. Even, it appeared, sacrifice himself.

It was a surprising feeling, this gallantry that had come over him. Surprising and bloody dangerous. The type of foolhardy action he would expect from Percival or Galahad. Not from himself.

The only good thing to have come out of this whole debacle was how Fionna was now sitting behind him, her arms wrapped around his waist.

Lancelot ground his teeth through the pain, trying to focus his mind instead of the feel of her breasts pressed into his back, the way her strong thighs moved beside his, the sweet yet herbaceous smell of her. Fionna's hot breath tickled his neck and his cock stirred painfully against his breeches. He muttered a muffled curse. So much for distracting himself.

"An inn," Galahad called out, pointing at the swinging sign that hung from a sturdy two-story timber and white-washed structure ahead. He let out a boom of laughter. "You'll love this. 'The Dancing Boar.'"

Lancelot hissed. "If I never saw another boar, it would be too soon."

"Are ye in pain?" Fionna's words were knitted with concern.

"What do you think?" he snapped.

He felt her stiffen behind him, and he closed his eyes against his stupidity. No need to take his frustration out on her.

"Serves ye right," he heard her mutter under her breath.

"What?" Lancelot asked incredulously, trying to turn to regard her with disbelief. But the pain exploded through his back and radiated through his legs, stealing his breath. A groan escaped his lips when his chest loosened, and he tilted in the saddle, suddenly dizzy and unsteady.

Fionna caught him, her arms circling him like a ship's rail, keeping him from plunging to his doom below. She reined Cheval to a stop before The Dancing Boar. "Can you hold yerself while I dismount?"

Lancelot grunted a nod.

Fionna swung down from his horse. "Galahad,

Percival, will ye help?"

Embarrassment warmed Lancelot's face as the knights helped him off Cheval and into the inn. The Dancing Boar's common room was a cheerful, tidy wood-paneled room filled with chatting and laughing townsfolk. A lute player sat by the hearth, plucking out a jaunty tune, and several couples spun and danced in the space before the yawning fireplace.

Lancelot tried to ignore the curious faces who peered at him as he sucked the breath in and out through his clenched teeth. The room felt too hot, and then too cold.

"All right," Percival said, appearing in front of Lancelot's line of vision. When had the lad left his side? "I secured us two rooms on the ground floor. Let's go."

Lancelot shuffled through the common room, much of his weight leaning on Galahad on one side, Percival on the other. In some corner of his consciousness, he saw the looks cast Fionna's way—appreciative . . . predatory. He wanted to face them down, to tell each man to place their eyes elsewhere lest they have them plucked out. But he was in no shape to intimidate anyone.

They pushed into the small room, just large enough for a two-person bed, a storage chest, and a little cupboard. Galahad and Percival lowered him down as gently as they could, but still the jostling sent stabbing pain through his body. "Easy," Lancelot panted, finally letting his head collapse back on the pillow. The bed was hard and lumpy, but it was blessedly still.

Lancelot opened his eyes and saw the other knights standing in a line, regarding him with worried eyes. "He shouldn't ride," Galahad was murmuring. "He likely bruised his spine or the muscles in his back."

"We need him," Percival said. "The standing stone said the blessed five."

Galahad frowned. "We'll have to wait."

"Arthur won't be happy about that," Percival murmured.

"Arthur can stuff it," Fionna said. Her voice grew soft. "But can Caerleon wait?"

"Quit talking about me like I'm not here," Lancelot practically barked. "I had a fall, I'm not dead. Give me more than five minutes to shake off the injury."

Galahad squinted his eyes. "His head seems in working order."

"And his attitude," Percival added.

"Should we find a chirurgeon?" Fionna asked. "Perhaps he could supply a tonic for the pain and swelling."

"Excellent idea," Galahad said. "I'll see if I can locate one. Percival, you see to the horses, and keep an eye out for Arthur?"

"Fine," Percival sighed. "But then I'm having an ale."

"Get me one of those too," Lancelot demanded hoarsely. A cold ale sounded heavenly.

Fionna pressed her lips together. "I'll stay here and make sure he doesn't do anything heroic."

"Little chance of that with the frosty reception I received last time," Lancelot shot back. "You're welcome, *Your Highness*."

"Oooh . . ." Percival's eyes grew wide.

"Let's leave them to it," Galahad said, pulling Percival from the room.

Fionna closed the door behind them, rounding on Lancelot, her hands on her hips. It wasn't fair to face her like this—her standing strong and proud—while he lay prone like an invalid.

"What do ye have to say for yerself?" she asked, crossing her arms beneath her breasts.

"I saved your life!" he shouted. "And nearly died in the process. I suppose it's too much to expect a little gratitude from the great and might Fionnabhair Allán."

"Ye didn't save my life, ye arrogant donkey!" Fionna shouted back. "I had the boar in my sights. I had a plan. I was ready for the beast."

"Apologies for not reading your mind, My Lady. What I saw was an eight-stone woman about to be trampled by a supernatural beast the size of two war horses!"

Fionna reared back, her smooth face darkening with fury. "That's all ye see when ye look at me? A frail woman who needs protecting?"

"No—" he protested, but she cut him off.

"Would you have pushed Galahad out of the way? Arthur?"

Lancelot bit his tongue. No, he wouldn't have. He would have trusted his fellow knights' training. But they knew the risks. They had trained for years. But so had Fionna, though not under his tutelage. So why *had* he felt the need to dive between her and the faerie boar?

"Curse it Lancelot, I'm a knight first, a woman second! When will ye get it through yer thick skull that I don't need ye to save me?"

Lancelot warred with himself, refusing to meet her sparking gaze. Bloody hell, he knew why. Hissing through the pain, he struggled to push himself to a seat. Some words shouldn't be spoken while lying down—this moment no different.

But Fionna was at his side in an instant. Her angry words were all but forgotten, gentleness and care taking resentment's place as she pushed him back down onto the bed. "Don't move," she said softly. "Ye could injure yerself worse."

Lancelot squeezed his eyes closed for a several heartbeats before meeting her piercing, silver-hued eyes. "I didn't push you out of the boar's path because I thought you weak, or female, or unable to defend yourself. I did it because . . . the thought of losing you terrified me beyond reason. I acted on instinct."

Fionna licked her lips as she processed his words. When she spoke, her voice wavered. "And do ye not think it terrified me to see ye lying there? To know not if ye were still alive? I have fought beside my brothers and sisters countless times, yet never did I know the fear I experienced today. If ye were dead . . ." A tear glistened at the corner of her eye, clinging to her white lashes.

Gods, she was beautiful like this. Raw and real, even more formidable in her vulnerability. Lancelot drew a hand up and cupped her cheek, wiping the tear with the pad of his thumb. Her skin was as soft as silk, as smooth as he had imagined.

She tilted her head into his palm, her eyes fluttering closed.

And then she opened them and reached out to brush a stray curl from his forehead. Her touch burned like sweet cinnamon, and their eyes locked. Sensations, as dark and sensual as a new moon, doused their fiery pulses with even darker desires. Fionna leaned forward, and awareness surged within him anew as her curtain of white braids swept around him, and then her lips caressed his.

Though the kiss was tender and sweet, almost chaste, her touch set his blood racing like he was a lad of sixteen, like this was his first taste of a woman. Energy and warmth surged through him, banishing each wince and pang from his thoughts, from his body. For what other sensation could compete with the feel of her? *Goddess, take me now.*

"Fionna," he murmured against her lips.

"I do not mean to lose ye, Lancelot du Lac," she whispered back. Fionna pulled away a few inches, her lips and cheeks flushed. "Not now, not ever."

Her soft words wrapped around his lonely heart, and he nearly started at the foreign feel of genuine devotion. Acceptance. Brushing her lips across his once more, she smiled before nestling gently against him, her head tucked against his shoulder.

Lancelot stared at the shadowed ceiling, stroking her silken hair. Her words echoed within him. No, she would never lose him. For Morgana had ensured that he would never be hers in the first place.

woke to Lancelot stirring beside me. His

Chapter Nine

Fionna

Ỻ warm presence was a comfort I was unused to enjoying; I had never slept beside anyone but Aideen. My heart spasmed painfully as I thought of my sister. Surely Arthur's messenger was already on his way to Lough Insholin to treat with Donal O'Lynn. I prayed Arthur's coffers were deep enough to secure my family's safety.

Lancelot's blue eyes blinked open beside me, and I banished thoughts of home. If I was to help my family, I needed to see this quest through. And to do that, we needed Lancelot well again.

"How are ye feeling?" I asked, laying a feather-light hand on his arm. I felt strange—touching him. As though I wasn't sure I could do so, that I wouldn't be scorned or have my head bitten off per his usual response toward me. But after last night's kiss, surely laying a hand on him was allowed, if not welcome.

Lancelot pushed himself to a seat gingerly. One hand strayed to his back, and he straightened his spine, twisting one way and then the other. "Better," Lancelot said, the word a sigh of relief. "Much better."

Galahad had found a doctor last night, but the man had been attending a woman in labor and promised to come when he was free. Apparently, it was a long labor, the poor woman.

Lancelot swung his feet off the bed and stood. He stretched, lifting his arms above his head until his back popped. "I feel like a new man."

Healing so quickly seemed a peculiar thing. How could he be so injured yesterday, yet be fine this morning? But, this miracle wasn't the strangest magic I had encountered since arriving in Briton. Not even this week.

A knock sounded on the door.

"Come," Lancelot barked. His eyes were bright, his color high. He seemed back to his old self. I shoved down a bubble of remorse for the loss of the sweet, quiet Lancelot I had lain beside during the night. *It was good that he was healed*, I admonished myself. We could now continue the quest.

The door opened to Arthur in a fresh tunic, his short hair ruffled as though finger-combed through with water. Shadows beneath his eyes spoke of a sleepless night, but his voice was cheerful. "You're up. From Galahad and Percival's description, I feared we would have to leave you."

"Fit as ever," Lancelot said, slapping himself on his broad chest.

Arthur narrowed his eyes, but there was a smile on his face as he said, "I suppose we have Fionna's tender ministrations to thank for your miraculous recovery? For surely you wouldn't have exaggerated your symptoms . . ."

I covered my chuckle with a hand. "I assure ye, Yer Majesty, if I ever catch the faintest whiff of any of ye trying to milk an injury for sympathy, ye'll be receiving a not-too-tender kick to the arse."

Arthur threw back his head and laughed, and the sound warmed me, making up for the icy daggers Lancelot was now shooting my way.

"Ye should have seen him last night. He could hardly dismount his horse. Lancelot is far too proud a man to fake an injury so severe."

"Are we done speaking of me as if I'm an invalid?" Lancelot asked.

"I don't know, what do you think, Fionna? Seems there are a few more jokes to be made."

"We don't want to hog them all though," I countered, sliding our dark knight a sly grin. "Percival would be beyond cross with us."

Lancelot threw up his hands, then began buckling on his sword belt. "What's the plan today."

"We're near Maesbury Marsh, where the bone carver lives," Arthur said. "We should pay her a visit before we head back to the main road."

"Who is this bone carver?" I asked.

"I am not sure exactly," Arthur said. "She is a legend. But if Merlin thinks she can help us, it's worth the trip."

"The Bone Carver is as mysterious as the Otherworld's mist," Lancelot volunteered, darting a glance Arthur's way. "Some say she walked the Earth before man was born. Some even believe humans are made from her very bones and that she still carves life into existence from the bones she gathers. Maybe Merlin believed she could carve us a talisman."

"Made from her own bones?" I asked, mouth agape.

Percival's ginger head popped around the corner. "How's crabapple doing? Feeling sour this morning? Though, not sure how you could be with such a lovely bedmate."

Lancelot scowled, and a blush rose on my cheeks.

"Has anyone thought of securing me a horse?" I asked, changing the subject. "Poor Aster didn't last long." I realized then how lucky it was that I wasn't riding Zephyr. I mourned any animal's death, but Zephyr would have been a blow to my very soul.

"We'll find one in the village before we head out," Arthur said.

The road north to Maesbury Marsh wound through thick forest, gnarled and old. The ground grew soggy beneath our horse's hooves, and the foliage began to change from the beech and ferns of the forest to the reeds and wildflowers of the marshland. Frogs croaked their warnings with every hoofbeat. Fireflies danced around the rushes and reflected off the blackened water—almost pretty, but they reminded me too much of will-ó-the-wisps, leading us to our doom.

"Not sure why anyone would want to live way out here," Galahad muttered, his eyes darting around the marsh and moss-draped tree cover.

"I suppose if you're a creepy old woman who likes to carve bones, a stinky marsh might just be the perfect location," Percival added, chipper as usual. How the lad wasn't nonplussed by the sights around him was beyond me. Then again, he grew up isolated in a forest with an eccentric mother.

"Shhh . . ." Arthur peered over his shoulder, then furrowed his brows. "She might hear you."

"Who is she, the Mother Goddess?" Percival quirked an eyebrow.

"We don't know how much farther," Arthur practically whispered. "We might be on her doorstep even now."

The knights fell into an uneasy silence at that, their heads swiveling back and forth, eyes peering into the marsh and to the shadows beyond. The smells of rot and brine tickled my nose.

I didn't see the moss-greened structure at first. The bone carver's cottage blended into the forest, so overgrown with roots and vines that the home seemed a living thing itself. A faded red door and the puff of wood smoke from the chimney were the only signs that this place belonged in the mortal realms.

Arthur dismounted first and the rest of us followed, a bit reluctant to make this woman's acquaintance. There was something ancient about the cottage—something *other*. The horses nickered nervously, stamping the ground as we tied them to a gnarled fencepost. An animal awareness shivered down my skin.

The door opened slowly, and within I could see only darkness, like peering into the throat of a great beast.

"Greetings," the woman said. Her voice was not that of an old crone like I had expected, but smooth and melodious. The lilting sound perked my curiosity to see her.

"Not often I receive visitors out this way. Please, come in."

One by one, we filed into the cabin, exchanging uneasy glances. Galahad placed a protective hand on the small of my back, as if to steady me. His touch stoked the fire within me instead. I missed Galahad. His strong hands, his honeyed kisses. I wanted to feel again what had passed between us—that and more. I stifled a sigh, trying to tear my thoughts from the emotion this man's simple touch could garner from me.

The cabin was much larger than it appeared from the outside, boasting one large circular room and holding all a person might need. A bed, a washbasin, a desk cluttered with papers and quills. Surprisingly mundane furnishings crowded one half of the space. But then there was the rest. Shelves of oddities—desiccated bodies of insects and small rodents and snakes. Jars of powders and liquids, whose purpose I couldn't dare imagine. And bones. Shelves and shelves of bones and teeth and skulls. The smell of the place was cloying, thick with smoke and a sweet odor that swirled about in my head.

"My name is Arthur Pendragon," Arthur began.

"Overking of Gwent. I have come to request your aid in our quest to find the Blessed Grail."

I could see her now, and was surprised by the woman's beauty, despite her age. Her sleek, gray hair was roped into a thick braid over one shoulder, her fine features delicate and elfin. She must have been extraordinarily beautiful in her youth. And now in her current age? She produced a feeling of wisdom and power. So much so, my hand strayed toward the sword at my hip.

"And what makes you think I can help, Little Dragon King?" the woman asked.

"My druid, Merlin," Arthur answered.

"Merlin?" she repeated, raising an eyebrow.

She had heard of him. Although I supposed most in this part of the world had.

"Who else have you brought?" she asked, turning her deep black gaze to each of us in turn.

"These are my knights. Galjorheledanik of Swansea, Lancelot du Lac, Percival of Caer Benic."

"Ah. A Fisher King. Perhaps you do not need my aid with him by your side."

"Och, I fear ye overestimate me, My Lady," Percival said. "Though . . . what should we call ye?"

"The Bone Carver." A smile played on her lips as she regarded Percival. "Or the Mother Goddess. Whatever you prefer, Grail prince."

Percival's Adam's apple bobbed as he swallowed thickly. "I meant no disrespect," he whispered, his brown eyes wide.

The Bone Carver turned toward me, and I could see Percival sag with relief from the corner of my eye as the weight of her attention passed from him. Icy fear crystalized in my veins. The woman stared as if she could see to my very core. My fears and doubts and shortcomings. All of them, laid bare.

"This is Fionnabhair Allán," Arthur said, "Princess of Clann Allán and the newest knight in my court."

The woman drifted toward me. Reaching out a hand out, she lifted one of my braids from my shoulder and examined my hair. I struggled to hold myself still, not wanting to insult the woman, but wanting desperately to be away from her. "An unusual knight," she mused to herself. "Very unusual indeed. You have power, fair Fionnabhair. Yet you do not use your magic. Why?"

My skin crawled beneath her scrutiny, and I buried my hands in the fabric of my tunic. "I don't know to what ye refer," I managed. "I'm a warrior. And a knight. I use those skills plenty."

The Bone Carver regarded me with an expression that I thought might be patronizing amusement. The searing gaze rankled me. What was this mad woman on about?

"Very well. You may keep your secrets. For now." She whirled to Arthur, and it was my turn to sag with relief. "You have brought me something. I can taste its magic in the air."

Arthur reached out to Galahad, who handed him a satchel. Our king then pulled one of the boar's tusks out and handed the ivory to her.

"These are from Twrch Trwyth. The faerie boar."

The Bone Carver took the tusk with reverence. "Oh yes, Arthur Pendragon. I will fashion you something from this, an object unlike anything in the mortal world."

"And this . . . object will aid us in our quest?" Arthur asked, his voice nearly breathless with excitement.

The Bone Carver nodded. "Do you have the other tusk as well?"

Galahad handed the ivory over to Arthur.

She regarded the two tusks with a wild gleam in her eye. "The second tusk will serve as payment. Are we agreed?"

"Agreed," Arthur said.

"You have come to the right place, dear knights. Wait and see what I shall carve you."

Chapter Ten

Galahad

Rain splattered across Galahad's unbound hair and shoulders as he stomped through the mud toward The Dancing Boar, the horses now bedded down for the night. The Bone Carver needed one more day to carve her object from the boar tusk. "Return tomorrow before the noon meal," she had said from her moss-draped doorway.

They had ridden into the yard behind the inn after the sun had set, a nightfall that was far too young. The strangeness was only confirmed when the innkeeper shared how they had departed five hours earlier. Yet the Bone Carver was only a thirty-minute trot from the inn.

Lightning flashed through the night air followed by a rumble of thunder. After kicking the mud from his boots, Galahad entered the inn and wiped the trailing raindrops from his face. If only he could shake his unease at the strange afternoon as easily.

Fionna peered up from a table near the hearth.

Firelight flickered in her gaze as she studied how his dampened tunic clung to his chest and stomach. Heat curled in his groin and flushed to his limbs. Their eyes touched for the briefest moment before she returned to her flagon of ale. He was glad to see how her spark and confidence had returned, especially when their king wasn't around. Arthur and Lancelot must have turned in for the evening.

Percival, noting his and Fionna's exchange, practically rolled his eyes.

Galahad slapped the backside of Percival's head and then fell into a seat right before the fire. "Fetch me an ale, lad."

"Fetch yer own, ye big oaf—"

"Need a drink?" A serving woman asked, leaning onto the table.

Her tightly-laced bodice fell forward, and gods. Large, soft breasts rose and fell in front of Percival's ale-flushed face. The kind of breasts a man could happily bury himself into and forget to breathe. Apparently, Percival had a similar thought. Galahad tugged on the back Percival's tunic to reel the younger knight back against his seat. Percival shot a look like daggers at Galahad, making him grin.

"Ale," Galahad said, pushing a copper across the table.

The barmaid pushed it back. "Free with a kiss." Her rouge-painted lips tilted in a seductive smile. Loose blonde curls fell over her shoulder as she eyed Galahad, her delicate eyebrow arched. "Or ale and a meal on the house, if you would like me to help you into dry clothes."

"I'll take a free ale," Percival chirped. Galahad still had a grip on the lad's tunic and held him in place.

Fionna cleared her throat and pretended to inspect her dagger, now in her hands.

"Just an ale," Galahad said with an appreciative wink. The barmaid pouted and then pushed off the table toward the barrels and caskets in the back. When she disappeared, Galahad released Percival's tunic.

"I'm not a wee lad." Percival scowled and shoved to his feet. To Fionna, he softened his voice, as if embarrassed, and said, "See ye in the morning, dove." And to him, "Ye get the floor tonight."

With that, Percival's lanky form marched from their table and down the hallway to the private two-bed room they shared with Fionna. Arthur preferred his second-in-command to keep guard when he traveled and rested in public places such as this. Though, Galahad thought it might be more from habit—the two had shared rooms since they were lads.

The barmaid returned and placed a large mug of ale before Galahad, gifting him another glimpse of her bouncing cleavage. Even he had to resist the pull toward falling into her bodice. Mayhap he was too harsh on his sword brother. Still, Percival was a strange dichotomy. Percival the warrior knight and Percival the sheltered young man from the forest. Odin's blessing, Galahad was well acquainted with maids by Percival's age. The young man should be allowed to play too. Sighing, Galahad eyed the half-empty mug of ale Percival had left behind and grabbed it, taking a long swig before gulping a few swigs from his own cup. Finished, he tipped back in his chair, resting his head, eyes closed, and enjoyed the warmth of the hearth.

"Ye're certainly pleased with yerself."

He cracked open one eye and focused on Fionna. "Not pleased. Warming up."

"Perhaps ye should change into dry clothes. Ye reek of horse."

A grin stretched across his face. "Strange how getting me out of these wet clothes seems of utmost concern to the fair maidens of this inn."

Fionna sheathed her dagger and then leaned forward on the table. A mischievous glint glimmered in her gaze. "I think I'll go keep Percival company."

His chair screeched as the front two legs slid back onto the floor. "And what do you plan to do with him?"

"Wouldn't ye like to know." Fionna downed the remaining dregs and slammed her mug onto the table. "See ye in the morning, *chipmunk*."

As she angled through the crowd of men and barmaids, he watched her narrow hips sway with each angry step—hips that fit perfectly in the palms of his hands. Hips that had once moved in rhythm to his. Galahad practically groaned as his cock stirred to life with the mere memory.

A man, deep in his cups, reached out and slapped Fionna across the arse. She whirled on him fast. The man didn't have a chance to blink before she slammed his head to the table, spitting next to his face.

"The next time, I'll cut off yer balls," Fionna hissed.

Men roared with laughter, a few cheered. Fionna slid Galahad a satisfied smirk and then waltzed away, down the hallway. To Percival.

Wait. Was that an invitation to join?

Oh gods.

In a flash, Galahad was on his feet and pushing through the crowd, his ale forgotten.

Fionna lingered outside his and Percival's door, and so Galahad stepped away from the lantern light and into the hallway's shadows. A few seconds later, Percival appeared, his mouth open with surprise. Before disappearing into their room, Fionna shot Galahad an impish smile.

The damn woman. Still picking a fight with him.

His long strides ate up the distance to his room in seconds. Without knocking, he pushed open the door and found Fionna and Percival in the center of their shared chamber, her lips pressed to the young man's, his arms practically limp on her waist. Was this Percival's first kiss? He didn't know. Nor was Galahad sure how he felt seeing Fionna kiss another. Jealous . . . or aroused?

Unaware of his presence in the doorway, Percival gripped Fionna's hips tight in his hands and tugged her against him. Fionna gasped and pulled back, her eyes wide, uncertain.

They stared at one another for a few erratic heartbeats, unspoken words passing between them. And then Galahad saw the shift, the moment Fionna looked at Percival, not with pity and surprise, but as a man who aroused her interest. Her fingers sank into his copper hair as her lips returned to his. And

Percival deepened their kiss, as if he were a seasoned expert. Galahad quirked a brow, resisting the urge to grin. But then Fionna's hands dipped to Percival's waist and begun unbuckling his belt and Galahad knew he needed to step in. She probably didn't know the rules of his vow.

"He might have a heart attack, if you go too fast," Galahad said, shutting the door.

"Come to chastise me, have ye? Not my fault yer ego can't handle that Fionna regards me as more than a chaste weakling." Percival glared at him once more. A strange look for their incurably happy knight.

Galahad smiled at him, not to mock, but in understanding. This was the challenge of a *man*, not a boy. And, if he were honest with himself, Fionna wasn't too much older than Percival. And he fully considered her a woman.

Fionna finished unbuckling Percival's belt and let it drop to the floor. The clanking sound filled the tense silence between them, until she asked Percival, "What do *ye* want?"

"Ye lass," he answered, breathless. "I want ye. But I fear I will want all of ye and I can't. Not yet." A flush colored Percival's cheeks and he twisted away, but she caught his face.

"Ye possess a strength the other men have not. There is no shame in yer sacrifice."

She leaned forward and delicately traced Percival's bottom lip with her tongue until he opened for her. Their kiss grew hungry and Percival moaned. A sound that pricked Galahad with guilt.

Her words shamed *him*, for she was right. All

this time, they had flaunted their freedoms in front of Percival and mocked his vow and the younger knight took it in stride, all smiles and laughter. Until this moment, Galahad hadn't realized that was a front. That a serious nature brewed beneath the cheerfulness. Because of the Fisher King's son, they might save Caerleon and Briton. Because of Percival, Fionna was alive and in this room.

Perhaps Percival was more of a man than any of them.

Chapter Eleven

Fionna

Percival's lips were soft and warm and beautifully reverent on mine. This other side of him, a serious side I had not expected, ripped the seals from my eyes. There was more to him than wit and boyish charm.

I had never quite payed attention to the deep timbre of his voice or the play of muscles along his jaw. Now, touching him, I realized he was far from soft and scrawny. Muscle and sinew stretched firm beneath my fingertips—formed from years of drills and fighting. And his eyes, gods his eyes. Up close, I could see every long coppery lash framing the rich, earthen tones. Eyes so brown, they were nearly black— sinful even. And his kiss? His mouth dancing across mine was akin to laughter and sunshine and . . . bliss.

His affections didn't hold the earnestness of Arthur's lips or the danger of Lancelot's kiss or even the seduction of Galahad's embrace. Percival was his own. Joyful.

A shadow of warmth sidled up behind me and my breath caught as I recognized Galahad, approaching even as my arms were twined about Percival. Galahad softly lifted my braids and kissed my injured shoulder. I shuddered beneath Galahad's touch and Percival gently pulled away at my reaction. Moons above, I had missed the honey-sweet of Galahad's touch, how he melted me to my core.

"Maybe," Galahad whispered, "we should show Percival the pleasures between a man and a woman."

"Ye mean—" Percival began but Galahad cut him off.

"You can't have sex, but you can watch."

Galahad's hands moved up my stomach and then cupped my breasts. His fingers were chilled from the cold of the night, a refreshing coolness on along my heated skin. My senses blazed into awareness as my head arched back against his chest, my gaze locked with Percival's. "What can ye do?"

"Kiss, touch ye." Percival swallowed as Galahad began rubbing the hardened tip of one my nipples with his thumb. "But I cannot be touched by another, ye ken?"

"Aye." My eyes fluttered shut. "Then watch for a spell and touch yerself. Join in when ye're ready. I won't allow ye to go too far."

"Two men?" Percival's breath came in quick. "Yer sure?"

"Does that bother ye?" I turned in Galahad's arms, nipping at his lower lip before peering over my shoulder at Percival.

"Nae lass." His eyes were bright.

"Then enjoy."

Percival sauntered over to his bed and fell back

against the pillows, unlacing his breeches and pushing up his tunic. Each nerve-ending I possessed ignited as I appreciated the ripple of stomach muscles under the candlelight, his eyes never leaving mine.

So many firsts flooded this space. The first time a man watched as I was pleasured by another man—a thrilling, daring prospect. The first time I would enjoy not one man, but two.

Wanting to arouse Percival farther, and eager for the forgotten taste of Galahad, I pushed up Galahad's tunic and licked at the raindrops still gathered on his pectorals. I wanted my tongue to carve fire across his damp skin. To sear his chest, his abdomen. From the corner of my eye, I could see Percival begin to stroke himself. At least the man wasn't shy.

I grinned up at Galahad, a predatory smile that I hoped relayed my message: I remembered last time. And I was going to make him pay. Galahad's dark blue eyes sparkled, silently accepting the gauntlet I threw down.

"How far do I have permission for?" Galahad asked.

"As far as ye like," I whispered back, gently biting his nipple.

A heady rush whipped through me as he flinched with the intended pain. Goddess save me, I wanted to bring this man to his knees. But not yet. No, the torment had only begun.

In one fluid motion, Galahad yanked his tunic over his head and then shook the water from his hair. I slitted my eyes when droplets hit my face.

"You're not wet enough," Galahad said with a

grin. Lightning forked across the night sky outside, lining the sultry angles of his face with streaks of white light. Thunder rumbled through our room. "Even the gods agree."

My fingers played with the laces of his breeches. "How do ye plan to appease the gods?"

He whispered, "I only want to please one," then lifted my tunic slowly over my head, tossing the garment to the floor. "A goddess."

Rain slipped down the latticed window panes and cast warbled candlelight across his already honey-toned skin. His chest was hard, everything about him was hard. I drowned in the feel of him, every line, every dip, the way his nipples rubbed against my palm, my fingertips, the way his muscles danced under my feather-light touch.

"Beautiful," Percival moaned from the bed. "So beautiful."

I glanced over my shoulder at the man, before turning to give him a better view . . . pressing my arse to Galahad's cock and slithering over his bulge. Galahad gripped my hips and moved me against him, achingly slow. Wanting to feel the anguish of every caress, I knew.

Percival watched, lips parted, his chest rising and falling with every flushed breath. Then the man's eyes dipped low and Galahad sucked in a breath as I slipped out of my breeches.

With Percival's eyes riveted to me, Galahad snaked an arm around my waist and trailed his finger down to my sex. I arched my back with a delicious moan. And so, he increased the friction, his finger moving back and forth. Percival shifted to sit on the edge of his bed, his own hand moving to the same rhythm. Galahad trailed kisses down my neck, to my shoulder, then he slipped his finger inside me.

"Oh gods," Percival whispered. His eyes watched Galahad move his finger in and out as his other hand played with my breast. The younger man's muscles flexed and tightened, his expression caught somewhere between ecstasy and lust. His lips parting farther when Galahad slipped in another finger deep within me.

Heat roared through my body and my knees grew limp.

I pressed harder against Galahad's cock, rolling my hips with each pump of his fingers. Wanting more. Needing more. Galahad turned my head toward his and he lowered himself until our lips crashed. My entire body sparked into a wild blaze. Every heightened sensation pulsed hot, a searing, liquifying pain I craved. Enough. I needed him on the bed beneath me. Now.

Apparently, Galahad felt the same.

He maneuvered to nudge me toward the bed, but I was faster. In a single move, I twisted him around and kicked under his calves until he fell on top of the covers. Galahad released a booming laugh. I knew he let me win. Just this once. And only because Percival was watching. Still, satisfied with myself, I crawled onto the bed with a wicked smile and tugged on his breeches until they slipped down his hips, down his thighs, and off onto the floor.

My heart stuttered to a halt. Galahad was surely

the most god-like built man I had ever beheld. Every inch of his body was sculpted to wondrous perfection. And he was mine for the taking. To destroy and torment and tease.

To love. And stars above, I loved him. I loved him and Percival both.

But part of me still wanted to win this round.

The length of Galahad's cock throbbed, and he nearly roared with release when I lowered myself down and swirled my tongue across his crown. He gasped my name, his chest heaving. My tongue would be the end of him, I was determined. Until he couldn't breathe. Until he clawed at the bed and tightened with building need. Then and only then would I pull away and give him what he needed. What I needed. Our eyes connected, and I flashed a taunting smile. Then my mouth slid down his length. Sweet agony burned each nerve-ending anew as he fisted my braids in his hands. Warm pleasure spread through my belly with his passionate response. My head moved up and down as he rocked his hips, groaning languidly. I could hear Percival's quivering breaths increasing nearby. The man's moans, too, as my tongue licked down Galahad's cock and back up, only to swallow him once more.

"Fionna . . ." Galahad choked out. "I am not sure I will la—"

He didn't need to finish. I crawled up his body, my hair brushing along the tightened muscles of his stomach and chest. And then I waited. Galahad's eyes snapped open as he adjusted his position on the bed. Fidgeting with desire for me. His hands running down the length of my back and settling, firmly, on my arse. Still, I didn't move, not until the glimmer in his eyes grew desperate, almost begging.

"Not a sound," I said right before I sank down onto him, until I felt his hips touch mine. Air hissed from his clenched teeth as he filled me completely. My head fell back with the intense feel of him, my eyes closing momentarily. My head buzzed and spun, dizzy with every hazy, soul-melting sensation. Then, with an impish smile in place, I lifted my hips up and hovered just above him. "No. Sound."

He reached up and curled a single finger around the infernal silver chain and lily pendant dangling from my neck. Then gently yanked until my lips collided with his. I could get lost and never recover in just his kiss alone. Releasing me, he closed his eyes and nodded his head in agreement to my terms.

Hot breath rushed from his lungs when I sank onto him again. With his nails digging into my arse and mine digging into his pectorals, I began to move. And not just move, I writhed as if I possessed him and knew it. One hand fell behind his head as the other moved from the soft flesh of my arse to cup my hip, pulling me back and forth to our fevered rhythm.

Galahad bit down on his bottom lip, hard, as if to keep from making a sound with each thrust. After several long, glorious heartbeats, he opened his eyes. I could tell he was watching me—the way my breasts bounced, the way my white-blond braids fell over my shoulders. The way the muscles in my arms and stomach flexed. His open appreciation and silent worship of my body brought me nearly to the edge.

But not as much as when Percival approached our bed.

Gods, these men made me feel so beautiful, so incredibly desirable.

I lifted my head toward Percival's, welcoming the heat of his kiss. Our lips danced to a soft, erotic melody. Then I arched my back, increasing the rolling motions of my hips. Percival knelt, taking my offered breast in his heated mouth. The most toe-curling moan I had ever heard left Galahad's parted lips. And I didn't know I could be anymore aroused. Percival blinked up drowsily from my breast before turning his attention to Galahad, brushing his fingertips along Galahad's ribbed stomach. Feeling how the man moved and rocked beneath me. Galahad stared at Percival, as if to warn the man that he wasn't interested. But Percival didn't notice, too taken with Galahad's body as well as mine. Then Percival returned his attention to exploring my breasts, cupping one in his hand while meeting my eyes.

"I want ye to be my first," Percival whispered between ragged breaths. "Once the Grail Quest is over."

I replied with a bruising kiss before whispering back, "I am yers." My eyes flitted back to Galahad's, nd I whispered, "And I am yers."

Galahad gripped my hip, grinding me against him, hard, frantic, saying, "I am yours. Always."

I didn't care if I lost control of this bout. Gods, I could lose every fight, if they destroyed me like this. Heat rolled between my thighs as my body clenched then rippled with a sensation so earth-shattering, I cried out.

Lightning flashed white in our candlelit room, illuminating our naked bodies. Then thunder cracked across the black sky, as if in reply to my release. The rain pounded on the glass. Percival continued to explore my body and kiss my swollen lips. Galahad lost himself to the delirium of my every touch and sigh. But me? I couldn't imagine feeling headier and more complete than I did now—to claim my knights and be claimed in return.

I was undone. And I never wanted to be put back together so long as I breathed.

Chapter Twelve

Arthur

rthur awoke to the steady pitter-patter of rain on the window and the cold pebbling of his skin. Lancelot hogged the covers. He had practically the whole coverlet bunched onto his side, wrapped around him tightly. Arthur pushed himself to a seat, elbowing Lancelot.

"Another few minutes, pumpkin," Lancelot murmured, and Arthur gave him another sharp elbow in the side.

Lancelot's eyes snapped open as a grin crossed his face.

"Awake you lump," Arthur said. "Bad enough for a king to share a bed with an unwashed man rather than a fair maiden. But you add insult to injury by stealing all the blankets!"

Lancelot stood, stretching over to touch his toes. "You have only yourself to blame, Your Majesty." How come when Lancelot said those words, it sounded a trifle mocking? "The innkeeper offered to turn someone out, so you could have your own room. But you are too damn gallant for your own good and didn't want to pull rank."

"Yes, well, with the storm . . ." Arthur murmured.

"They would have put them up with the horses. No one would have been caught in the rain. And as for the fair maiden, our fifth knight would likely leap into bed with you, if you would only start talking to her again." Lancelot slid him a mock-flirtatious smile. "That's an easy conquest, even for you."

Arthur rubbed his face to clear the sleep, ignoring the tightening in his breeches. "Yes, well, if the sounds coming from the other room had anything to say about her interests, I'm too late." The rumble and clap of thunder had deafened most of the noises emanating from the other knights' room, but there were a few telltale moments that Arthur couldn't argue away as his imagination. It had to be Fionna and Galahad. The damn Dane was far too brawny and handsome. Arthur combed his fingers through his hair. "God knows what poor Percival did to drown out the sound. Perhaps he put a pillow over his head."

"Or perhaps he partook," Lancelot raised an eyebrow, lacing his boots.

Arthur raised an answering eyebrow, pausing as he reached for his sword belt. "Partook? But the Grail Quest—"

"I'm not saying he bedded her, but there are . . . *things* a man can do short of the full deed."

Arthur's face flushed at the possibilities. He knew Lancelot was relaxed about his own sexuality as well as sexual experiences—from his youth with the faeries. But the very thought of one woman with two men was new to Arthur. And alarming. Though, if he were honest, a touch arousing. He cleared his throat, pulling on his boots. "And you think Fionna would be willing to enjoy the company of two men?"

Lancelot shrugged. "She mentioned how women in her clann often take two or more husbands. And that she feels something for several of us. *Definitely you*. She has been beside herself since she betrayed you. And she'll do anything to win back your favor."

Arthur furrowed his brows, buckling Excalibur around his waist. "I don't like the thought of Fionna laying with me simply to win back my favor. I would have her choose me freely, not to appease some sense of obligation or duty."

Lancelot rolled his eyes, letting out an exasperated breath. "Will you stop being so noble, man? All I'm saying is that *she cares for you*." He pushed a finger into Arthur's shoulder. "*You*, Arthur Pendragon. She's holding back because she fears *you* are still angry with her. If *you* show her that you're not, she'll come to your bedside gladly."

Perhaps Lancelot was right. He had been holding himself back from Fionna since she had stolen Excalibur. But was he truly ready to open his heart to her again? He wasn't sure. But if he didn't now, perhaps he would lose her—Galahad would stake his claim—and then when Arthur finally came around, he would be too late. "Wise counsel, my friend. But, I thought you possessed no favor for Fionna. Now you think we can trust her?"

Lancelot buckled on his cloak. Something foreign flashed through his eyes—something shadowed that Arthur couldn't quite place. What was it about the two of them? "Fionna . . . she's not for me. That doesn't mean she's not for you." He clapped Arthur on the shoulder. "Now let's go get whatever creepy-as-hell bone thing the witch carved for you."

Arthur laughed. "Can't wait."

The road back to the Bone Carver's cottage was much as it was before. The rain had mostly stopped. Fat drops slid off the leaves above them, finding their way onto foreheads and down tunic fronts not protected by their cloaks. Arthur liked the smell of the air after a storm—as if the whole world was fresh and rejuvenated. If only the curse could be vanquished as easily.

Arthur rode by Lancelot and Fionna rode behind with Percival and Galahad. Those three warriors were gleeful as maidens around a Maypole, chattering and laughing, the color high on their cheeks. Envy snaked through him, its green fingers grasping at his heart. He wanted to make Fionna laugh like that, to put that sultry, knowing smile on her face.

Lancelot cast a sideways smirk his way. "You keep sighing like that, you're going to run out of breath. Just go talk to her. Tell her you forgive her. Fully this time, and not just because you need her on the quest."

Arthur stifled another sigh. "I hadn't realized my thoughts were so plain."

"A goat is better at keeping secrets than you."

"I don't know, a goat can be sly. They steal the washing off the line and eat it . . ." Arthur said, frowning.

"Fine." Lancelot threw up his hands. "A chicken. A chicken could lie better than you."

Arthur chuckled. "A king needn't do everything himself. Perhaps you can serve the roll. Be my royal deceiver. Whenever I need a lie told, I'll send you in—" He fell silent as Lancelot's face grew blacker and blacker.

"As you wish, Your Majesty," Lancelot said stiffly, before kicking his horse into a trot and pulling ahead.

"Lance—" Arthur called out, cursing his un-thoughtful jest. Lancelot must still be sensitive over the business with Morgana and the two serving-wenches. Would he never be rid of his half-sister's foreboding presence?

Arthur went in alone to retrieve the item the Bone Carver had created for them. Curiosity warred with wariness as he entered her house again while the others awaited him outside.

"Little Dragon King," the woman said, a smile

curving her face as he entered. "I have something quite magnificent for you."

"I could hardly sleep last night from the suspense," he admitted.

"You sure it wasn't the pounding?" the Bone Carver said, the smile growing wider.

How could she possibly . . . "What?" he asked, his mouth going dry.

"Of the weather," she clarified. "The storm was a loud one."

"Yes, the storm. Perhaps thunder and rain contributed."

She pulled a box off a shelf—the size of his two palms together—then she handed the plain, carved wood over to him. "Open the lid."

Arthur swallowed as the hinges creaked. Inside lay a key. Milky white, carved of bone. The craftsmanship was exquisite, the key's bow an intricate triskelion knot of intersecting lines. "A key," he said. He fought disappointment. He didn't know why, but he had expected a dagger, or a staff, or something that wasn't . . . a key. "What does it open?"

"The door will reveal itself to you when the time is right," the Bone Carver said.

Of course. Another faerie riddle. Anything to do with the Grail was full to the brim with intrigues. He nodded. "I thank you for your aid. The craftsmanship is superb." He closed the lid and bowed. "Now, if I may beg your leave, we must be on our way. The journey is long, and time is of the essence." He turned toward the door.

"Don't you want to ask me your question?" she

asked after him.

Arthur spun on his heel. "What question . . ." he trailed off. But he knew what question and straightened. "You said my knight Fionna had power. What power do you speak of?"

"I know not. The truth of her is shielded from my sight, for a reason I cannot discern. But this hidden magic is a mystery worth exploring."

His shoulders drooped slightly. He didn't know why he had thought this strange woman could tell him something about Fionna. And he didn't know exactly why he thought there was something to tell. Only what he already knew: there was indeed something unique about his fifth knight. And as the woman said, a mystery worth solving.

"I will offer you this advice, Arthur Pendragon, free of charge. Keep her close to your side. For she is the other key you need on this quest."

Arthur ducked his head in thanks. The Bone Carver's words followed him out the door. Another key. But to unlock what?

Chapter Thirteen

Percival

Nothing ruined a ride through the countryside like coming upon a dead body. Percival's mood that day had been buoyant, to say the least. Ecstatic might be a fairer description. He couldn't stop thinking of Fionna—the look of her taut stomach in the candlelight, the feel of her bare breasts . . . his cock grew hard with each lingering thought. The way her eyes had fluttered shut in pleasure as Galahad took her. As soon as this quest was over, he would show her such pleasure. He was surprised at how little he had minded sharing the experience with Galahad, though part of him wanted a woman all to himself. Wanted a night with *Fionna*—all to himself.

As the latter thought ignited him once more, his horse danced to the side beneath him—the movement so sudden, he was nearly thrown.

"Och," Percival groaned as he caught sight of what Kit had avoided. "Arthur!" he called back. "Ye need to see this." They were deep in the territory of Gwynedd. Though, not technically Arthur's kingdom, his role as the Pendragon together with his generally honorable nature meant the problems of other Welsh lands still weighed heavy upon his king's conscience.

The knights gathered around the poor fellow, who had been horribly mauled from the looks of it. Must have been a gruesome way to die.

"This just happened," Fionna said, a pale hand before her mouth. "Less than a few hours ago, I would say."

"What manner of creature did this? A wolf? A boar?" Percival asked, looking about.

Lancelot muttered, "Not another bloody boar."

"Look at these tracks," Galahad said, kneeling in the crushed grass, just beyond the man. "They don't look like wolf or boar." He frowned, placing a hand down next to the prints. "There are almost—fingers. I mean, clawed fingers. Five on this print . . ." he rolled in his bottom lip while thinking. "Four on this one. I've never seen anything like these marks." He stood.

"The tracks seem to lead in the direction of that lake," Fionna pointed. "Could the creature live in the lake?"

"But why didn't the creature take the man with it? Or eat him?" Lancelot asked. "Could this mysterious beast kill for sport?"

"There's a village round the other side of the lake." Arthur pointed just ahead of their trail. "The poor fellow likely belongs to someone there. Let's take him back for burial, and then find out what they know about the beast behind this vicious attack."

etws-y-Coed was a quaint town much like one would find in Gwent. Squat, lime-washed houses topped with thatched roofs and bounded by tidy vegetable gardens. As they rode slowly through the main thoroughfare into the cobblestone circle at the center of town, the faces of townsfolk followed them with curiosity, rather than hostility. Even when they dismounted.

A man strode out of the only large building in town, which professed itself to be the village inn. "We welcome you," the man said. He was barrel-chested and tall, nearly bald, but with strong features and a confident way about him. "I'm Willum, the Manor Lord of this village. What brings you to us?"

"Arthur Pendragon, Overking of Gwent," Arthur said, and Willum bowed hurriedly, his brown eyes going wide. Those eyes flicked over each of the knights in turn, settling on Fionna with startling intensity. Percival frowned.

"My humble apologies, Your Majesty. I did not see a king's banner or I might have graced you with better manners befitting your crown."

"At ease, Willum," Arthur held out a kind hand. "We were traveling nearby and came across a man who had been slain. We feared he may be a man from Betws-y-Coed and thought only to deliver him back to his family." Arthur motioned to Gala-had, who gently pulled the man's body off the back of his horse, lowering him to the ground. They had wrapped him in a spare cloak, but blood was seeping through the fabric.

Willum's hand strayed to his bare head in an un-conscious gesture. "Another one? Bloody hell." He winced, seeming to realize his words. "Pardon, Your Majesty."

"Another one?" Percival asked, stepping up. "He isn't the first?"

Galahad knelt and pulled the cloak back, reveal-ing the man's identity.

Willum's face fell. "Yes, he's one of ours." A semi-circle of townsfolk had grown around them, and Willum turned to a lad who was hanging back. "Jon, go fetch Roselyn, will you? Tell her to bring her sister. Be gentle about it."

The boy nodded and dashed off down the road.

"I'm afraid he isn't the first. A monster lives in our lake and stalks the good people of our town. And I fear within the month, a town won't be left to find."

"A monster?" Percival asked. "What nature of creature? Have you seen this beast?"

Arthur cast him an annoyed look, but he couldn't help his curiosity. Wasn't it every knight's duty to slay the beasts preying on innocent Welshmen and women like this?

"The beast is called the Afanc," a lilting female voice answered.

They all turned to where the voice had come from and Percival's eyes widened at the sight. On the fringe of the circle stood two women—unlike women he had ever seen. Their hair shone black as midnight, their skin tawny and bronzed. With tilting eyes framed by dark lashes and full, voluptuous lips, the two women were some of the most beautiful creatures he had ever laid eyes on. Excluding Fionna perhaps—though the beauty of these women was of a different type altogether. Sultry and foreign. Their attire was stranger still, colorful silken fabrics flowing around them, tied about their tiny waists. Curved swords rested at their hips and gold glinted in their ears and . . . even in a woman's nose!

"And who are you?" Lancelot asked, lifting his piercing blue eyes her way. Percival suppressed a snort. Nothing drew Lancelot out of his black mood like a beautiful woman.

"I am Cyra," said the one with the nose ring. She was shorter, fuller of hip and bosom. "And this is my sister, Lelah."

The other sister had long silken hair that cascaded down to the small of her back; she wore a necklace with a ruby the size of a robin's egg. The women must know how to use those swords, if they felt safe to ride about alone with such jewels on their person.

"We have traveled from our home of Constantinople, tracking the Afanc," Cyra added. "The creature was born of dark magic in our land and, therefore, it is our duty to kill this monster."

Cyra knelt by the man who had died, and placed a hand on his chest, closing her eyes. Then she looked up at Willum and shook her head. "I'm too late."

Too late? Percival thought. It was plain to see the

man was dead, but Willum seemed crushed. His face fell even more until deep lines crinkled his eyes and around his mouth.

Lelah spoke, her voice soft as a rose's petals, "We are grieved how the creature made it so far, killing so many. The Afanc has taken to this land's cold climate, and so we have bound it to this place, to keep the monster from moving on. If we have any chance of ending this beast, it will be here."

"Your cause is noble," Arthur said, nodding. "But it's only a beast. Surely with all of you together, you could make quick work of it?"

"This is no ordinary beast," Willum said. "It has magic and controls the river somehow, making the water overflow beyond the banks with devastating results. Our farms have been flooded time and again. We'll have nothing for winter."

"Even magical creatures can be slain," Galahad said.

"Not this one." Willum's grief-stricken gaze met Galahad's. "All the Afanc does is kill. Again, and again."

"What do ye mean?" Fionna asked.

Lelah spoke, laying a gentle hand on Willum's drooping shoulder. The man suddenly looked exhausted, as though he had never known a day of sleep in his life. "To keep the creature sated, each day Willum and his son and daughter go down to the pool where it lays in wait and sacrifice their lives to the monster."

Percival recoiled, and the other knights exchanged shocked glances.

Arthur spoke first. "How do you still live? And what do you mean, each day?"

"The creature isn't hungry," Willum said. "It just wants to kill mortals. So, we give it something to kill. And then Cyra and Lelah bring us back to life."

Lancelot's brows furrowed over his darkening eyes. "What sorcery is this?"

"Our magic is similar to the type that crafted the Afanc," Lelah said. "The connection between this place, the creature, and these people—it enables us to do what no man or woman should be able to do. Bring back the dead. It was a solution for a time, but we cannot continue indefinitely. We haven't been able to end this cycle."

Excitement was building in Percival. This was a perfect opportunity to prove his worth—to Arthur, to Fionna. He knew last night had been a step toward her seeing him not as a mere lad anymore, but as the man he was. But slaying this beast would cement this truth in all their minds. Plus, these poor townspeople needed relief. A hero.

Percival straightened, lifting his chin. "The monster must die. And I will help ye slay the Afanc."

Lelah's face softened. "We thank you for your offer, brave knight, but I am afraid it would be a death sentence. For the Afanc cannot be killed by any mortal weapon."

Arthur stepped up beside Percival, casting an exasperated look his way. "If that is the case, then I believe we can help. For my blade is not forged by a man."

Chapter Fourteen

Fionna

I couldn't help but think of what a strange world I had tangled myself up into by joining Arthur and his knights. In Ulster, there were goddesses to honor before battle and whispers of faerie tales around the hearth fire. But here, in Wales, the extraordinary seemed an everyday occurrence.

I noticed the stiff set of Arthur's shoulders as Percival boldly announced how he would valiantly slay the Afanc. Then how the frown on Arthur's shadow-lined face deepened as he reluctantly agreed to Percival's heroics. But I knew my king's bleeding heart, and we would not have ridden from this hidden village without helping her suffering people first. It wasn't in his nature to be calloused or indifferent.

"There are rooms enough in the inn for each of you," Willum said, tugging me from my internal ramblings. "Don't have a lot of visitors these days. Get settled, Your Majesty, and then we can talk further at dinner."

I turned to lead my new horse to the stables—a

dark earthen brown gelding named Acorn—when Galahad strode my way, intent upon me. My breath hitched in my chest as I beheld him, as the heat of memories billowed in my blazing pulse and curled throughout my body. The exquisite feel of him inside me, all around me. Skies above, he was a singular pleasure unlike any I had ever known. And with Percival there beside us, his hands and his lips upon me . . . I was more daring than I had ever been, but our shared intimacy still felt so very right. Even now, I reveled in the sensations of my body, the sweet soreness between my legs.

All these thoughts flashed in the space of a second. But Galahad pushed past me gently, laying a hand on my shoulder before he leaned down to lift Acorn's hoof.

I craned my head around the bulk of his torso and pressed my lips into a thin line. The shoe was loose.

Galahad clucked his tongue in disapproval, straightening. He patted Acorn's sleek shoulder. "He was favoring this foot during the latter part of the ride," Galahad said. "Willum! You have a farrier?"

Willum nodded, pointing toward a wattle and daub structure at the end of the village. "Blacksmith can shoe a horse."

Embarrassment prickled at my flushing face. "I should have noticed." I prided myself on paying expert attention to my mounts. They were partners and friends. But apparently, I had been too wrapped up in my thoughts over my knights to notice. Once again, I found these men were changing me. Some of my new differences I liked, but other alterations I found quite unwelcome.

"Don't worry." Galahad shrugged and leaned in, his body heat and sandalwood scent threatening to destroy what was left of my good sense. "I only noticed," he whispered in my ear, "because I was admiring how nice your arse looks in a saddle."

I replied with a snort of outrage, but my heart wasn't in it.

Galahad gave my chin a little tap with his knuckles before sauntering away to join Arthur and the others who conversed with the eastern mystics. The beautiful, seductive, compelling magical mystics with hair as black as onyx and skin as smooth as buttermilk.

I shoved down a tendril of jealousy as I led Acorn toward the forge. What was I afraid of? That Arthur or his knights would fall for one of the women? They were free men, I had no claim to them. But even as I said those words to myself, they rang hollow. I had laid claim to each of them, and them to me. Even the-ever-insulating Lancelot, who seemed inexplicably determined to resist the dark, passionate bond that was germinating between us. Already, the building steam began escaping his tamped-down control. My lip curled in disgust, and I kicked a pebble with the toe of my boot. I would not be one of those women who schemed to keep a man through tricks or jealousy. If I wasn't compelling enough for the likes of them, then I was better off without their fair-weather hearts.

The blacksmith was a rugged man with arms as large as Galahad's. He kept his black hair cropped close to his scalp, and his thick beard neatly trimmed.

His eyes widened at my and Acorn's approach, and he laid down his hammer to straighten his apron.

"My Lady," he said, inclining his head. He had a pleasant voice, deep and honest. "How may I assist you?"

"My horse's shoe is loose," I said. "Left front. Do ye have time to re-shoe?"

"It would be my honor, Lady." He took Acorn's reins and then felt down his fetlock toward the shoe. "I am called Colwyn. What brings you to Betws-y-Coed?"

"I am Fionna," I replied in kind. "We were passing through when we found . . . one of the Afanc's victims. I believe my fellow knight is going to try to help."

"Help?" Colwyn lay a hand on Acorn's neck, stepping closer to me. His eyes darted to the necklace around my neck and then, slowly, his gaze traveled back to mine. "Are you the maiden?"

I wrinkled my brow. "I'm not sure what ye mean."

He took another step closer and I stilled my hand's twitch toward my sword. I didn't think he was being threatening. If anything, the glint in his dark eyes as he regarded me was—reverent? He smelled of sweat and woodsmoke, iron and musk. Honest smells.

"You've met the mystics?"

I nodded.

"Well then surely they've shared that there is only one way to lure the Afanc out into the open. The creature is partial to fair maidens. And you, My Lady, may be the fairest of all."

My mouth opened and then closed in surprise.

Men had complimented me before, but few were so forward. "I thank ye," I managed. "If a maiden is needed to lure the Afanc out to be killed, then I suppose I can volunteer. Now I'll leave ye to your work and return when ye're finished with Acorn's shoe."

I unbuckled and pulled my saddlebags off Acorn's rump quickly, grateful for their bulk before me.

"Fair Fionna . . ." Colwyn's voice caressed my name and a chill clawed its icy fingers up my spine. "I am a man of few means, and surely you could sup with gods and kings, but if you would have me—"

"I thank ye for yer kindness, sir."

I backed up hastily out of the forge's heat. Then I spun on my heel, my mind working furiously as I hurried toward the inn. The man offered me his hand in marriage! What manner of madness was this? This town was growing stranger by the minute.

Night fell quickly over the little village. Willum had served us a mouth-watering stew flavored by spiced rabbit and carrots and turnips, the remnants sopped up with warm, hearty rye bread. The farm ale was naturally chilled by the elements and light, just as I preferred my hard drinks. I was now feeling comfortable and drowsy as I leaned back in my chair, my mind drifting comfortably in the way only a good meal can inspire.

Willum was blowing out the candles in the far corner of the common room while sweeping the floor.

"We should retire," I said. When had the hour bloomed so late?

"Indeed," Arthur said, pushing to his feet. "Lord Willum, thank you for the fine meal. Please give your daughter my esteemed regards for her culinary skills."

The innkeeper and Manor Lord paused from his tasks. "If you can rid us of the Afanc, you've free meals here for life, Your—"

Galahad stood. "I accept your generous offer."

"Not you, good Sir." Willum grinned, an odd look on his sorrow-lined face. "You look as though you could eat a wagonload each meal."

Galahad guffawed at the man's audacity, and the rest of us laughed as well. I wanted to help these people. They had spirit, despite their current circumstances.

Lelah, the woman with the long flowing tresses, appeared in the stairwell's doorway. She had changed into a dress of cobalt silk that left little to the imagination. "My sister and I desire your company. To share more about the creature. Will you come?"

Arthur nodded and followed Lelah up the stairs, followed quickly by the others. I pursed my lips before joining the invitation.

And stars, the sisters' chambers were unlike any I had ever seen.

"Remarkable." Percival goggled, his head swiveling back-and-forth to take in all the extravagance.

The familiar-styled furniture I knew lined the side walls to make room for a dozen large, colorful pillows, each cushion carefully positioned over a vibrant-patterned rug. Tapestries stitched with gold thread hung on the walls, and brightly-hued lanterns in octagonal shapes cast strange symbols all around the warmly illuminated room.

"Welcome," Cyra said, kneeling on a pillow before a roaring fireplace.

"You brought all of *this* with you?" Lancelot surveyed the room, wrinkles appearing on his forehead, his mouth tilted halfway between a sneer and a frown.

"Home is so far away. The endless distance is difficult at times. So, we thought to bring a bit of home with us," Lelah said, as if carrying all of one's home furnishings across the known world was perfectly common.

"Pity the mule who had to carry your treasures," Lancelot muttered, and I stifled a laugh, grateful for Lancelot's cynicism to break the spell of this bewitching place.

"This is cozy." Galahad plopped onto a pillow by the fire across from Cyra, toeing off his boots.

"No, beautiful . . ." Percival whispered. But his eyes weren't fixed on the room. They were fixed solely on Lelah.

I started to sigh but stopped when I caught Lancelot watching me. A calculating look glittered in his icy-blue gaze—a shadow of a smile on his sensual lips. With just a single look, I felt naked before him—I knew he had undressed my thoughts—could see my petty jealousy. Arthur, Galahad, Percival, Lancelot—these incredible men were mine. But I hadn't claimed them. Not truly. Not in a way that was binding.

The smile broke across Lancelot's face in earnest as he strode forward, dropping onto a cerulean-hued cushion beside Cyra. "We thank you for your hospitality, dear sisters," Lancelot practically purred at her, each sultry-spoken word frothing my blood into action.

I narrowed my eyes at him and his smile grew wider, his scintillating eyes locked with mine. Oh, so that's how he wanted to play?

My good sense fled me as I slinked onto a beaded cushion between Arthur and Galahad. Closer to Athur than was strictly required. Let the games begin.

Chapter Fifteen

Fionna

"May we offer you refreshments?" Lelah peered up through her lashes at the men—a look both demure and coy. In one hand, she held a blue glass bottle that I assumed contained some sort of alcohol and, in the other, a finely carved bowl.

Lelah settled onto a cushion between Percival and Arthur as Cyra stretched back and retrieved a tray with glasses from a low bookshelf.

Lancelot examined her arched form with unveiled interest, and I rolled my eyes.

The sisters poured a clear liquid into the tiny glasses and passed them round. I studied mine, marveling in the glass's beveling and the gold inlay. They were chalices a queen might drink from. I couldn't fathom how these beautiful vessels traveled unimaginable leagues and remained intact.

"My gods!" Galahad exclaimed, regarding his empty glass—he had already downed the contents. He blinked rapidly. "That tastes of . . . anise."

"Anise?" I asked, sniffing my drink. "What is anise?"

Cyra laughed, a light, carefree sound. "Pace yourself, good Sir. Even a man such as yourself will feel the effects of Arak, if you drink so quickly. Arak is strong." Cyra turned her gaze onto me. "Anise is a spice native to Constantinople, where we are from. Sultans and Pharaohs, even the Greeks and Romans, have enjoyed drinks and candies made from anise seeds and licorice root for ages."

"The Welsh Lord who squired me would travel to Rome every so often," Galahad shared. "He returned with licorice and anise candies for his household each time."

Lelah was attending to the bowl now, lighting the end of a little wrapped herb bundle in the fire. "Breathing in the vapors of the dried cannabis plant is tradition in our land. Before battle. This medicinal herb will help you relax and sleep deeply. This is the least we can do to honor and prepare you for tomorrow."

"We thank you, My Ladies," Arthur said, taking a sip from his glass. "But what would also help prepare us is more information about the Afanc. You said this creature comes from your land. What else can you share?"

"The blacksmith shared how the Afanc is only lured out of its lair by a fair maiden. Then the creature begins to kill," I added. "I offered to serve."

All the knights' heads swiveled my way. I shrugged.

"I am only being logical. I can defend myself."

Though a horrible thought struck me. Hopefully by maiden he meant young woman and not . . . an actual maiden, as in virgin. After what Galahad and Percival and I had done last night, I certainly didn't qualify in the latter sense. Remembered pleasure shivered over my skin, and I took a gulp of the drink to down the memory. The liquid burned my throat, the powerful taste of anise filing my nostrils. I coughed. "Arak is . . . interesting," I managed, hoarsely.

Galahad laughed.

"Arak isn't for everyone," Cyra said sweetly.

Lelah was waving a graceful hand through the pungent smelling smoke now, wafting ribboned tendrils in lazy curlicues.

"Lady Fionna speaks truth," Lelah said, setting the bowl on the carpet between us. "The Afanc requires a fair woman to bring the creature out into the open. But there is something else you must know. The Afanc is invisible."

Lancelot froze mid-sip and coughed. "I'm sorry, is that a joke?"

"We're afraid not, Sir. But," Cyra said hastily, "we have a talisman to help."

She reached across Lancelot's lap, flashing him a flirtatious smile, and then retrieved a little box by the fireplace. The lid was carved in geometric designs and inlaid with mother of pearl. Here in Wales, a treasure such as this box would fetch a king's ransom. Or in Ulster. The latter thought burrowed deep into my mind. And, with a painful pang, images of Father and Aideen tormented my grief. Surely Arthur's messenger was drawing near the shores of Ulster by now. My stomach heaved at the memory of my own voyage across the Irish Sea. A sailor I was not.

Cyra opened the intricately-carved box to reveal a small, green, rough-cut gemstone. "This is an adder stone." She offered the talisman to Percival. "If you are the warrior who will face the beast tomorrow, then this stone is yours to carry."

Percival took the gem, turning the stone over and examining the colors in the light. "I would like to remain the warrior, lass. But . . . His Majesty's sword possesses the power to slay the beast, ye ken? Perhaps . . ." He turned to Arthur, hope in his brown eyes. "Perhaps I could borrow your blade, My King?"

Arthur frowned, his hand straying to Excalibur's hilt. He seemed to consider, wearing the face of a king, rather than the boyish one I preferred. Finally, he nodded. "I will lend you Excalibur to complete this task. Just don't run off with my sword." I froze as Arthur slid a sideways look my way. Relief flooded me when a hint of a smile appeared at one corner of his fine mouth.

I let out a shaky laugh. "Indeed. For what kind of knight runs off with their king's sword?"

"A treacherous one," Lancelot muttered, robbing the moment of all its levity. I resisted making a lewd gesture at him as he scooted closer to Cyra.

"May I have more of that liquor?" Galahad held his glass out as I took an experimental breath from the bundled herbs.

"So, tell us of this Afanc's creation, My Ladies," Lancelot said, his voice smooth and sweet. "You mentioned how the creature's magic mirrors your own? How can that possibly be true?"

Lelah wound her thick hair into a braid as she began to regale us with stories of how their mentor, a great mystic in Constantinople, explored dark magics. Her voice was melodious and mesmerizing, the story hanging in the air before me as if a moving tapestry. I could feel the heat from the desert's beating sun—though, I knew not of what a desert truly was or looked like. A land of endless, golden earth and sparse vegetation? It boggled the mind. I could smell her mentor's bubbling cauldrons as Lelah spoke them into life in the room, and I could also see the glint of gold and scarlet of their master's turban, which Lelah demonstrated by using a scarf. So many wonderous new words and images. I was riveted.

Sweat trickled down my back and I pulled at my thick tunic. I was so hot—my limbs heavy and pleasantly numb. The sweet-smelling smoke seemed to fill my head, dulling my senses. I unbuckled my sword belt and pulled off my boots. Against the backdrop of the story, I was dimly aware of the movement in the room—Galahad pouring himself another glass; Percival's fingers trailing up Lelah's arm and around her swan's neck; Lancelot pulling Cyra onto his lap, his strong hand tangling in her black tresses, his lips brushing along her collarbone as she arched her head back in delight.

Jealousy coiled in my stomach, until I noticed Arthur next to me. He had removed his crown and his boots, though not Excalibur. He was gazing at me with such a look of plaintive longing that his ardor, his open desire lanced through the fog in my head and pierced straight to my heart. My king . . . my king still *wanted me.* Even after all I had done—the treachery, the betrayal. I knew what that sleepy, dreamy look meant in a man's eye. And seeing Arthur's face softened so? An answer to a prayer I dared not express even in the shadows of my heart.

The room faded away as Lelah finished her story, and I grabbed a fistful of Arthur's tunic and pulled him to me with more strength than I realized. He toppled forward and we both tumbled back onto the pillows with a surprised laugh and soft, pleasurable exhales of breath.

The others peered our way in surprise at the sudden motion—Percival's lips plump from kissing Lelah, Lancelot turning from the half-untied laces of Cyra's gown. Galahad—well Galahad was snoring softly, passed out in a pile of cushions, his arms and limbs spread out.

Arthur pushed himself back up and tugged me to my feet. "I thank you for your hospitality this evening, My Ladies. I fear I must retire."

"I am tired as well," I managed, though I'm not sure who I was trying to fool.

Lancelot's eyes darkened before he turned back to Cyra, burying his face between the curves of her full breasts.

I shoved aside my unease at the sight and grabbed my boots and sword belt. Then, I allowed Arthur to tow me by the hand to his chamber two doors down.

Once inside, he pushed the door shut, walking me back with the bulk of his body until my spine pressed to the door. My breath hitched as his lips met mine, strong and sure and *Arthur*.

". . . My Lady . . ."

"Arthur—"

"—Do you—"

I couldn't give my consent fast enough. "Kiss me. Touch me. I give ye permission to do as ye please."

Arthur pulled away just enough to meet my eyes. "I do not wish for you to think I only long for you after imbibing in tonight's exotic offerings. Nor as a guilt offering." He cupped my face with a sweet, chaste kiss. "I have behaved the fool," he whispered hoarsely. "I ache to bridge the distance I selfishly created between us."

I traced my fingertips over his lips and whispered back, "I wish for you to only know pleasure and happiness, Arthur Pendragon."

His eyes fluttered shut as an appreciative shudder wended down his body. "I need you, Fionnabhair Allán."

"I am yers, My King. My heart, my mind, my body, I give it all to ye this night. Whatever ye need of me."

His lips were upon mine, this time slow and reverent. The back of his fingers caressed the curve of my cheek and down my neck. Light touches that betrayed his trembling hands and his quivering breaths. As if he were holding back an enormity of emotion. As if he knew apologies and requests for forgiveness were trite compared to the words his heart wished to express instead. No man had ever touched me with such veneration and my knees grew weak at the beauty he made me feel with just the tips of his fingers and the soft stroke of his lips.

Pulling back, Arthur took my hand in his and led me toward the bed. Candlelight flickered across the walls and glinted in night-blackened latticed window. A blush colored his fair skin as he glanced at me shyly over his shoulder. The authority of a king had melted away to reveal a vulnerable young man, a boyishness I couldn't resist. Longing pooled deep in his gaze as he cherished the very sight of me, and I found myself flushing as well, as though a bashful maiden instead of a fierce warrior. Our awareness of one another charged the air between us. An energy both bright and beautiful. A deep connection I could not explain yet felt all the same, as sure as I breathed.

At his bed, Arthur leaned in and pressed his lips to mine once more. This time with building urgency. A firestorm burst between us and my hands roamed the broad expanse of his chest, shoulders, and back, needing to explore the searing flames licking our bodies. The heat was utterly delicious, the headiness more blissful than the finest wine. We fell to the covers and tangled into each other's embrace, our clothing and armor tossed about the floor.

His breath shuddered as I began kissing the freckles across his chest and down the ribbed muscles of his abdomen. Hard muscle formed a tantalizing V down his hips to his groin and my mouth needed to savor every dip and curve of his masculinity. The soft caress of his fingers on my face, the feel of his skin on my lips, the moans of pleasure escaping his mouth, the way every sculpted line of his body flexed when the tip of my tongue tasted the salt of his excitement—they were a far more intoxicating drug than the one we had enjoyed earlier this evening.

I licked the length of him, my core burning for release as he breathed my name . . . as though a prayer, as though a plea. As though my name formed the very breath in his lungs. To draw out each sensation intensely, my mouth slid down the shaft of his cock achingly slow while my tongue swirled across the sensitive skin. His hands left my face to grip the headboard and his hips rolled beneath my ministrations. And then they rocked again, slow at first, but quickly gaining rhythm as his breaths grew more ragged.

"Fionna . . ." he called out as his body stiffened until the veins in his forearms stood in stark relief. I leaned back to watch him climax, a smile on my lips as he groaned, muscles tightening and then relaxing. He was the most beautiful man I had ever known, even more so when he peaked.

I crawled up the bed to his mouth, wanting him to taste himself on my lips. His kiss was deep, erotic, and breathless. More sensual than I expected of Arthur. Then he rolled me onto my back and, with a grin, cherished me in return. And gods, the feel of him as the hard planes of his body brushed along the soft curves of mine, as his tongue played with my nipples before dipping to my thighs. The fire blazing hot and licking our bodies now pooled between my legs, and I burned with each sizzling flick of his tongue. I wanted to turn to ash in his fingers, to feel the earth quake beneath me. The pleasure built and billowed as he lapped at my arousal until I cried out, clutching his hair, then the covers, then the head-board behind me.

Arthur moved up my body and buried his face into my neck. He trailed light kisses down to my collarbone, then to my shoulder. "We are fated for each other," he whispered into my skin. "My body belongs to yours. I am your servant and gladly kneel before you."

He grazed his nose along my jaw, his hot breath branding my skin. With a sigh, my head fell back, and my eyes closed while the moon kissed my pulse and glittering stars danced in my veins.

"I love ye, Arthur Pendragon."

"I love you, Fionnabhair Allán."

Chapter Sixteen

Percival

Percival felt different with Excalibur on his hip. Stronger. Invincible. Was this how Arthur felt all the time? He didn't think so. Perhaps the weight of Arthur's crown balanced out whatever joy he might gain from this faerie blade. Lately, his king walked with a mantle of worry about him that seemed to grow heavier by the day.

With a sigh, he squinted his eyes and peered down the trail.

According to Lelah and Cyra, the Afanc slept in a slow-moving stretch of river just past the village, where the water rippled in lazy circles against an expanse of flat stones.

The thought of Lelah set Percival's blood racing. His head still felt filled with wool from last night's spicy drink and strange ceremonial smoke. His memories were etched in hazy images that were as slippery as eels. He knew he hadn't broken his vow last night. Indeed, he thought he had only put the skills he had gained with Fionna to good use. Glimpsed memories of Lelah's caramel skin and the sound of her soft moans as he saw to her pleasure tantalized him. She was an exquisite woman. But . . . Percival glanced at their fifth knight out of the corner of his eye, walking beside him through the forest, her face peaceful. Lelah had been like a pleasant dream, but only a dream. Elusive as their herbal smoke. Fionna was real. What he had felt when he had touched her—when her lips had burned across his skin—the solid presence of her at his side and in his life. His night with the mystic had confirmed one detail in his mind. For him, there was only Fionna.

"Ye have the stone?" Fionna asked, for the third time.

"Aye, dove. I didn't lose it between the village and here." Percival pulled the stone from his belt pouch and tossed the talisman into the air, watching as the rough-hewn facets sparkled in the morning light.

"I just want ye to be prepared. This beast has taken down many men. And the mystics can't bring us back, like they do the villagers."

"Ye know, lass, if I didn't know better, I would say ye were worried for me." A smile quirked at the corner of his mouth.

Fionna looked at him with a mixture of care and exasperation. She reached out and grabbed a fistful of his tunic, pulling him sideways against her. She then tucked herself under his arm in a way that Percival found extremely pleasant. "Of course, I'm worried for ye. I am fond of ye, Percy. Ye must promise ye'll be careful. No heroics."

"Percy?" he asked, a grin forming.

She arched a white brow. "What, ye think yer the only one who can hand out nicknames?"

"Fair point, lass."

"So, ye just have to hold the stone?" Fionna asked. "And the invisible and secret will be revealed to ye?"

"According to Cyra, it really is that simple." He felt Fionna stiffen beneath him at the mention of the mystic.

Percival softened. "Ye know . . . last night meant nothing, right? Just idle fun. For Lancelot too."

"It's none of my business who ye bed with." Fionna focused on the ground, a muscle in her jaw jumping.

"If ye say so." Was Fionna jealous? The thought filled him with a bolt of gleeful excitement. "Ye know there's only one lass I want to be with . . ."

Fionna remained silent.

"It's ye," he added.

She rolled her eyes, pushing him away from her. "Yes, I gathered that, ye goat."

Percival laughed, but as he did, his eyes caught something strange about Fionna. He blinked, then squinted in case the streaming sunlight was playing tricks with his eyes. But the strangeness was still there. A web of delicate silver filaments covered her from head to toe—as though Fionna had walked through the gossamer strands of a bejeweled spiderweb.

"What?" Fionna asked. "Ye're gaping at me like a fish."

"There's . . ." he hesitated. Did Fionna know she was covered in a web of magic? Why had he never seen the signs before? A sudden thought occurred to him and Percival shoved the stone back into his belt pouch. As soon as his fingers broke contact, the shimmering lines disappeared. He pushed out a shaky breath.

"Fion—" he began, but she shushed him.

"There's the pool." She pointed. "Hide yerself. I will go from here alone."

Percival retrieved the stone again from his pouch, ignoring the strange lines resting over Fionna's fair form. He would deal with that mysterious magic later. Now, the Afanc needed to be his sole focus. He slowly pulled Excalibur out of its sheath, reveling in the surge of energy flooding up his arm.

"Be careful, dove," he hissed in warning as she crept toward the riverbank. She held a dagger near her hip, but her sword wasn't out. She didn't want to frighten the Afanc.

Percival crept closer, pushing through the trees to find a better vantage point.

Fionna reached a large flat rock on the riverbed, its granite face dappled by the sun. She settled upon the top, her dagger gripped beneath her bent knee. And then she began to sing.

Percival's mouth fell open as the first notes of her melody reached his ears, borne gently on the spring breeze. Her voice was as clear and pure as the rushing waters beneath her, sweet as honey mead. A lullaby. Perhaps one that was sung to her when she was wee bairn . . .

> *O sleep my wee babe, under the rowan,*

With the sun repairing
With the moon in her silver chair in
Watches with your mother
Too-ra-la-la, Tra-la-lo...

He closed his eyes, allowing the sound of Fionna's voice to wash over him, to permeate his very soul. He hadn't thought their knight could be any more magnificent a woman than she already was. But this new gentle facet of her only made him love her all the more.

A tear dripped from the corner of his eye and crawled down his flushed cheek. He wiped away the moisture hastily as he opened his eyes, sniffing.

And then he recoiled, only just keeping himself from crying out in alarm. For resting its monstrous head in Fionna's lap was a creature more hideous than he had ever encountered before. Long and sinuous, covered in dark gray scales, the Afanc's long flat snout brimmed with sharp white fangs. Its eyes, set on either side of its grotesque head, were closed.

Fionna continued singing but was gesturing wildly, pointing to her lap, her eyes white with fright. Percival nodded, creeping out of the trees. What a sensation it must be for Fionna, feeling the weight in her lap but not being able to see the creature's form. Or perhaps cradling an aggressive monster was easier this way.

Her voice wavered but she cleared her throat quickly, taking a deep breath before launching into another verse. The creature stirred briefly but settled again as the notes rang out, flicking its meaty tail in contentment.

Percival leaped onto the rock where Fionna sat, landing as gently as he could. He froze, watching the creature with predatory grace. The Afanc didn't move, lulled to sleep by Fionna's sweet tune.

Fionna made a stabbing motion at the beast, followed by one that could only translate as: *get on with it.*

Percival felt a pang of regret as he crept closer. Seemed a shame to end a creature that enjoyed Fionna's song as much as he . . . but the Afanc had killed and would kill again.

When he stood mere inches from the beast's outstretched claws, he raised Excalibur's shining form, aimed at the beast's spine, and plunged the sword point down.

The Afanc exploded in a fury of pain and gnashing teeth. Fionna rolled out of the way, launching herself off the rock and into the shallow river below.

Percival pulled Excalibur free and swung it in a deadly arc, slicing through the creature's neck to the spine. Black foul-smelling blood welled from the monster's dismembered parts. The Afanc's violent death throes—its scaly tail whipping across the rock—knocked Percival's legs out from under him. He tumbled backwards, rolling awkwardly down the side of the rock and into the stream next to Fionna.

With a spluttering shake of his head, he righted himself, pushing to his feet.

The monster had fallen still—dead.

Fionna grinned, splashing water at him. "Percy, Briton's most graceful monster slayer."

"Och, ye're going to pay for that, ye goose." Percival shoved the stone back into his pocket and Excalibur in its sheath. And then he ran for her, tackling her back into the pool over her shriek of protest.

"Percival!" Fionna sputtered, pushing her braids out of her eyes. "I'm soaked!" She narrowed her eyes at him before splashing him full in the face.

Percival laughed, opening his arms wide. "Go ahead, lass. Hit me with yer best shot!"

Fionna cupped her hands in the river and doused him.

"Nice to see you two are enjoying yourselves," a dry voice came from the riverbank.

Percival and Fionna froze, then slowly turned toward Arthur. The other knights were emerging from the trees, followed by the mystics and Lord Willum.

"All in a day's work," Percival said cheerfully, quickly adding, "Yer Majesty."

"That blade better not get any rust on it," Arthur called out.

"Faerie blades can't rust," Percival said. "Right?"

"You sure about that?" Arthur arched a brow, crossing his arms before him.

"The Afanc is really dead." Lord Willum stepped out onto the rock, regarding the bloodstained rock with an expression of shocked delight. "You did it! You killed the beast!"

"Well done, brave knights," Lelah said, her beautiful face beaming at them. "You have freed this village, as well as me and my sister, from this creature's terrible hold. How can we thank you?"

Percival stepped up onto the rock, pulling Fionna

up after him. "As knights of King Arthur Pendragon, High King of Briton, it is our call to help those in need. No thanks necessary, My Lady."

"Please," Cyra said. "We must give you something."

Percival unbuckled Excalibur and passed the sword back to Arthur, relieved as the weight left his side. He pulled the adder stone from his pouch and offered the talisman back to Cyra. "This relic was invaluable. Thank ye."

"Keep the adder stone." Cyra pushed his hand back. "I have a feeling our talisman may aid you on your journey."

Percival looked at the glittering facets, thinking of the strange lines over Fionna's features. "If ye're sure."

"Where do you travel next, fair knights?" Lelah asked.

"To Castellum Puellarum," Arthur answered. "Traveling along the River Conwy will be the fastest route to the Irish Sea. There, we'll sail to the Port of Ayr, journeying across Strathclyde and into Alba. We need to avoid Anglo-Saxon territory as much as possible, save Castellum Puellarum, of course."

Fionna blanched. "Wait . . . did you say sail?"

"Would you rather face Anglo-Saxon armies by crossing through most of Mercia and Northumbria?" Arthur tilted his head, his eyes studying her face.

She grimaced. "A battle I can fight. But my stomach doesn't care much for boats."

Chapter Seventeen

Lancelot

Lancelot trailed behind the others as they rode toward the port town of Conwy. Arthur and the other knights were in high spirits since leaving Betws-y-Coed, after enjoying the hospitality of the mystics and slaying the Afanc. They had freed a village of a monster and Percival had secured for them an invaluable relic.

He glanced over at the handsome young man, his heart faltering a beat at the impish smile pulling on Percival's lips. The lips he sometimes found himself thinking about kissing. Maybe one day he would work up the nerve.

Lancelot heaved a shaky sigh and returned his attention to the river trail. He should feel as celebratory as the rest. But a black cloud hung over his mood, one he failed to banish.

The frosty look Fionna had been leveling at him all morning didn't help, either. Well fine. If she was offended, then he could be upset at her too. He wasn't the only one who enjoyed the comfort of another last night. Fionna hadn't claimed him personally. He didn't belong to her beyond mutual duty to their king and land.

He had wanted to believe that a night with Cyra was exactly what he needed to rid Fionna from his mind. The mystic was beautiful, intriguing, and powerful—and talented in the art of lovemaking. But as he lost himself in the caramel skin of her neck, her dark obsidian eyes, the shimmer of gold from her nose ring—the colors had been all wrong. His traitorous mind kept sliding to thoughts of silver and white—the silver of beech bark on a still winter's day, the soft gray of a dove's feather. And as he laid beside Cyra after their lovemaking ended, Lancelot had stared at the ceiling, wondering what Arthur and Fionna were doing in that very moment.

It was good, he told himself. Good for Arthur and Fionna to be together. If she was Arthur's lover . . . she moved one step farther from Lancelot. Yet another reason why she was untouchable. Never mind that she had apparently ruined him for all other women. That was his burden to bear.

"So, let me see this adder stone," Galahad said, interrupting Lancelot's internal rants. "This talisman will make the magical visible?"

"That's what the mystics said," Percival said. "Certainly worked on the Afanc."

"That beast was hideous." Galahad shuddered.

Lancelot privately agreed. The beast had become visible to all upon its death. The creature was an unnatural horror.

"Ye didn't have that monster laying its bulbous,

scaly head in yer lap!" Fionna said as Percival handed over the stone to Galahad. The copper-haired knight seemed hesitant to part with the stone.

"I can't blame the creature," Galahad murmured, holding the adder stone up to the light. "You have such an appealing lap."

"That doesn't mean my lap is open for any man or beast who would like to nap!"

Arthur laughed. "The Afanc certainly had not heard that edict."

"I don't know, Percival," Galahad said. "I'm not seeing anything magical."

"Oh?" Percival asked. There was a hint of strain in his voice that Lancelot couldn't account for. "Perhaps we are in a distinctly un-magical area."

"Ah, here's a sign for Conwy," Arthur said.

They had reached a junction in the road, and a sturdy wooden post announced the directions and mileage to several nearby villages. "We're just a league away."

"What language is *that*?" Galahad asked, squinting at the sign. "I've never seen the likes before."

The others looked at him.

"Which sign?" Fionna asked.

"The bottom one. With all the squiggles."

Lancelot exchanged a look with Arthur.

"The bottom one announces the distance to Llandudno," Arthur said.

Percival shot Galahad an impish smirk. "Perhaps that licorice potion guttered yer mind."

"Or the cannabis smoke." Fionna blew out a breath. "That stuff was especially strong."

"I'm not addled." Galahad pointed. "Right there. Under the marker for Llandudno. There's another sign." He looked incredulously at the others as they shook their heads and shrugged.

"Give me the stone," Percival said.

Galahad handed the relic over.

Percival's eyes widened. "I see it too! Nae, he wasn't addled, he was addered!" He hoisted the stone for all to see with a cheeky grin.

"Wow," Lancelot muttered as Arthur pinched the bridge of his nose. "That was terrible."

"Clever," Fionna offered weakly.

Galahad playfully glared at Fionna. "Don't encourage the man."

"Can you read the language, Percy?" Fionna asked.

"Percy?" Galahad cackled so loud a flock of birds roosting in a nearby tree burst into flight.

"Yes well," Percival cooed, "just because ye don't warrant a Fionna nickname isn't a reason to be jealous, chipmunk."

Galahad opened his mouth to retort, but Arthur silenced him. "Can we get back to the magical sign, please?"

"Right. I can't read the language," Percival said, handing the stone to Arthur.

"Appears to be a form of faerie script," Arthur said. "Lancelot?"

Lancelot took the stone from Arthur. The talisman was warm and heavy in his hand. When he looked up at the sign-post, he saw what the others were referring to. Below the placard for Llandudno was another sign etched onto what looked like hammered silver. Lancelot urged his horse closer and peered at the writing. "Faerie runes. The language of the Túatha dé Danann. The sign says . . . 'Percival is an idiot.' Huh, I guess this unfortunate truth is becoming common knowledge." Lancelot raised an eyebrow at their mischievous knight.

"Har har," Percival said, throwing a lewd gesture at him.

"Can you read faerie runes?" Arthur asked Lancelot.

"It says, 'Caer Benic, 95 leagues north and 31 leagues east.' I think they're coordinates."

Arthur's eyes lit up. "Truly? Directions to Caer Benic? Here?"

"Must be another message from the Grail Maiden!" Percival said, practically falling off his horse in his excitement. "Like the stone circle! She is leaving clues for us to follow."

"Appears so," Lancelot said, handing the stone back to Percival. As their fingers touched, warmth traveled up Lancelot's arm. Percival's eyes snapped to his and he drew in a quiet breath. Aware of other eyes upon them, Lancelot retracted his hand and busied himself by chipping away at a piece of dried mud on his saddle. Then he remembered. The instant before he handed over the stone, he thought he had seen something shimmering around Fionna. But then the stone passed from his fingers, and Percival's touch stirred him, and now he wasn't sure if he had imagined the vision around Fionna.

"But we're going by sea," Fionna said, tugging

Lancelot's focus back to the present. He slid Percival a furtive glance before resting his attention onto Fionna. "So, how will this distance help us?" she asked. "Perhaps we'll have to go overland from Conwy?"

"No such luck, My Lady," Arthur said softly. "We travel north to the Kingdom of Strathclyde, across from Ulster, actually. The Anglo-Saxons would revel in my captivity, if we port farther south or travel by horse across the isle."

"If we can find a map and estimate the distance from Ayr to Castellum Puellarum," Galahad reasoned, "we could then use those figures to determine how far Caer Benic is from our eastern Strathclyde destination."

Arthur nodded. "I thought the same thing myself. Perhaps our search will still be a needle in a haystack, but this should narrow our quest down to the right haystack, and keep our party safe. Let's keep riding while the sun is in our favor." Arthur kicked Llamrei into a trot.

They reached the port village of Conwy in no time.

Lancelot reigned Cheval behind Fionna's mount as they walked onto the crowded wharf, full of fishmongers selling their latest catch and merchants loading or unloading vessels.

"My steward has arranged a vessel to take us to Ayr," Arthur said, nudging Llamrei forward. "We're looking for the Scarlet Selkie."

"Sounds like a fun ship," Galahad said with a soft laugh.

"No ship is a fun ship," Fionna countered. She

was looking even paler than normal.

Galahad quirked an eyebrow. "Am I to understand that our fair Fionna isn't a sailor?"

"If the goddess intended for me to float on water, she would have made me a swan," Fionna muttered.

"Ye would be a very handsome swan," Percival said.

Fionna wrinkled her nose. "No one looks handsome while retching over the side of a boat."

Lancelot tried to hide a smirk.

"What are ye looking at?" Fionna asked him, her eyes flashing in challenge.

"It gives me comfort to finally discover one thing that you are *not* good at."

"There are plenty of things I'm not good at," Fionna shot back.

"Such as?"

"Understanding brooding French princes."

"I share a similar weakness in trying to understand the whims of murderous Irish princesses—"

"There she is," Arthur said, interrupting them. He pointed to a sturdy vessel with a hull painted in red ochre.

Fionna turned from Lancelot and closed her eyes. She seemed to be muttering a prayer. Whether it was for an iron stomach or patience, Lancelot wasn't sure. He could use the same divine aid.

Chapter Eighteen

Arthur

Arthur had never really trusted the sea. The land was firm and solid and reliable. But the sea? Ever-changing and unpredictable. Always moving. Even on a calm day, unfathomable life teemed beneath the surface. Creatures of this world and unnatural monsters. An entire underwater realm he didn't understand and would never see. It didn't help that in a single blink of the eye, that strange life could turn on you, swallowing you into its abyssal depths.

Perhaps the sea was akin to loving a woman. Though with Fionna, he had glimpsed beneath her surface—or so he thought. Regardless, she was a woman he dearly wanted to understand. Like a sailor takes to the sea, learning Fionna might take him a lifetime of trying and failing, learning and exploring. With Fionna, it would be a life well lived.

The captain of the Scarlet Selkie was a short stocky Welshman with a brown shaggy hair and a weathered face so furrowed you could plant crops in the wrinkles. Davies ran a tight ship—his crew was tidy, respectful, and hardworking. On this clinker-built cog and the two others carrying their horses and supplies, Davies was king. And Arthur could respect a man who fairly ruled his domain.

For three days now, they had been at sea and would port this day. Fionna spent the better part of these three days with her head over the side. The warrior hadn't been jesting. She truly was seasick.

They took turns sitting beside her in a nook the five of them shared at the longboat's stern, regaling her with tales when the ship's bard wasn't on duty. They shared stories of brave deeds or foolish ones.

Except Lancelot.

Lancelot had taken up a position on the longboat's bow and appeared as fixed and as firm as the ship's selkie masthead. He stared out over the sea, watching the endless waves, the soaring gulls, and the craggy coastline of Wales and Strathclyde pass by. Arthur had thought Lancelot was surfacing from his black cloud, but his mood seemed to be declining further instead. Arthur sighed. He had resisted talking to Lancelot, knowing his friend was just as likely to bite his head off when he got like this. But . . . maybe he could help, nonetheless.

Arthur walked across the boat, past coiled ropes and sailors, to stand by Lancelot's side. "You aiming for a record?"

Without turning Arthur's way, Lancelot grunted, the sound more like a question.

"How long a man can stand and look at the sea?" Lancelot shot him a sideways look. The gray of the sea reflected in his light eyes, turning them a smoky hue.

"Oh no, you broke your streak." Arthur flashed him a crooked grin.

Lancelot rumbled out a dark laugh. "Not much else to do on this vessel."

"You could help us keep Fionna company. She's asked after you."

Silence.

"Did something happen between the two of you?" Arthur asked. "I thought . . . I don't know. I thought things were better."

"Don't you ever miss how things were? When it was just the four of us?" Lancelot asked.

"I—I don't know. Things can't stay the same forever, Lancelot. We were always going to add more knights."

"More knights, yes. But with Fionna . . . nothing is the same." A gust of frigid wind teased Lancelot's curls and Arthur wrapped his cloak more tightly about himself.

"We're still the same, Lance," Arthur said, using his nickname from when they were younger men. "You and I? We are brothers."

Lancelot turned to him, and the pain in his friend's eyes nearly stole Arthur's breath. "We'll never be the same again. Not since Morgana. And certainly not after Fionna. My friendship with you is the one possession I treasured most in this world. And now our brotherhood is the one thing I fear will never be the same again."

Arthur set his jaw. "Different, yes. But let us

make our friendship stronger, then. Allow these adversities to bring us closer. I feel like you are giving up, and I don't know why. If this is about Fionna, my friend, my *brother*, I have been thinking much on what you shared. The time she spent with Galahad and Percival doesn't bother me so much as I thought it might. Perhaps . . . there is room for all of us in her heart. Even you."

"And in her bed?" Lancelot's lip curled, his dark eyebrows knitting together.

"Even in her bed. If that is what she wishes . . . I think . . . I think I might be warming to the very idea."

"You mean, *brother*, that you will put up with anything because you are so desperately in love with her?"

Arthur's pulse darkened. "I *mean*, each of you is dear to me in a way I cannot express. Our fellowship is precious to me, and even more so now that Fionna has joined our brotherhood. Somehow, she has completed us. But this completion doesn't feel right with you on the outside like this. And I don't understand why you insist upon separation when I am insisting that you are welcome. And needed."

Lancelot buried his face in his hands, scrubbing at the morose, haunted shadows lining his face. "You deserve happiness Arthur Pendragon, more than any man I have known. With me in the mix . . . things could only implode spectacularly. It is because I love you, and I love her, and I love Caerleon that I will hold myself apart."

Arthur whispered, "I do not understand . . ."

"Someday you will. And you will thank me." Lancelot twisted away from Arthur and resumed his post as before—his mind lost at sea.

Arthur waited several heartbeats before walking stiffly back to the ship's stern, ducking his head and studying the planked floor beneath his boots. Emotions roiled within him. His friend had proved an enigma even since they were lads. But lately . . . Arthur heaved a tight breath as heavy and chilled as the North Wind. Perhaps being raised by the cursed faeries darkened Lancelot's tongue. He had learned their ability to speak truth without saying anything decipherable whatsoever.

As Arthur pushed past a sailor to his party's corner nook, the smell of sick hit him like a top wave, turning his already soured stomach. Fionna lay on the sea-drenched floor, shivering, her head resting on Percival's thigh—the lad asleep—with an extra cloak draped over her weakened body. She hardly looked up when he lowered himself against the rail boards. Her face was pale and coated in a sheen of sweat, and her arms wrapped around a wooden slop bucket.

Galahad stood, giving Arthur a little more room. "Going to stretch my legs," the big knight said. Arthur didn't blame him. This ship was oppressive.

"Thank you, friend," Arthur said. "And you, Fionna? Would you like to try and stretch your legs a bit too? Might help you."

She moaned, her eyes fluttering. "The only thing helping me," she rasped, "is this strange little root Lelah gave me." She held up a piece of gnarled brown root in her hand. "Chewing on this actually soothes my stomach."

"What did she call it again?" Arthur reached out to examine the root, but Fionna snatched the strange plant back, as if it were the most precious possession in the world.

"Ginger," Fionna managed. "Oh boy," she shoved herself up onto the rail, jostling Percival awake while positioning herself over the sea.

Arthur stood and pulled her long tresses and braids off her sweaty neck and out of the way. Then he placed a comforting hand on her back and drew soft, soothing circles. With his head, he gestured for Percival to go stretch and walk with Galahad. The young man complied, but only after a hesitant look Fionna's way.

She breathed out slowly, sagging in relief. "False alarm, I think."

"Do you desire another story?" Arthur asked, settling back onto planked floor beside her.

"You have any left? I think Percival has exhausted all the Scoti tales he knows, and Galahad the Norse ones."

"I have a few left to share. Do you want the one about the knight and the green man or the knight who befriends a lion?" Arthur asked

"Do all your stories revolve around knights?"

"Obviously, they have the best adventures."

A ghost of a smile flickered across Fionna's face. "You choose."

"All right. Once, a king was hosting a feast. A huge green giant showed up and offered to let someone cut off his head with an axe, so long as he could do the same to them one year and a day later—"

"That doesn't make any sense," Fionna countered, her eyes closed. "The giant would be dead."

"They're legends Fionna. Details don't need to be plausible."

"Right," she whispered.

"Are you going to listen?" Arthur asked. "Or are you going to argue?

"Argue . . ." she whispered faintly in reply once more, but her body had grown still.

Arthur brushed loosened strands of hair from her cheek. Her pale, waxen face finally appeared relaxed, the lines of tension around her eyes and mouth now peaceful, her breathing even.

Arthur gently pulled the bucket from her grasp, wincing when she stirred. But the motion had not awakened her, and she settled back into much-needed slumber.

He placed the bucket on the other side of where he sat and then pulled an extra wool blanket slowly up over her, softly kissing her clammy brow. "Rest fair Fionna. Dream of green giants and solid shores."

Chapter Nineteen

Galahad

early five days had passed since arriving in the Kingdom of Strathclyde. One day of rest in the grand port city of Ayr, followed by four days of hunger and growing weakness while skirting around musty peat bogs and crossing through endless birch, pine, and oak lined woodlands. Forests and marshes that should be teaming with game, but strangely remained shrouded in pale, misty silence. The trees and grasses had withered into shades of brown and gold, odd colors for this rain-soaked land. Black sap oozed from trunks and limbs and oiled the surface of every bog they passed. Galahad's horse, without grass or grain for leagues now, dragged each hoof over yet another hill.

So many hills and rock formations. He didn't know the land rose to such heights and so willingly until he had ventured into Scoti territory.

But nothing compared to the hunger gnawing at Galahad's stomach, like a wolf that slowly chipped away at the bones of its last kill. His fellow sword-brothers fared no better, and Fionna even worse. The poor woman was but a husk of her former self. After three days of purging all nourishment from her body, she was barely present at times. Her silver eyes frosted over from a dull, persistent ache he knew she felt in the deepest recesses of her gut. Her skin shimmered in the chill as though ice crystals. Yet, she held herself aloft in the saddle with nary a complaint. A warrior even when flirting with the delusions of hunger, even when shivering from the never-ending mist.

A moving, almost living mist that appeared deep in the forest, several leagues east of Ayr.

He thought back to the day they had reached port. Striding across solid ground had warmed Galahad's dampened spirits after so long at sea—strange for a Norseman, he knew. Still, the earth had felt strange beneath his boots, his legs unsure of how to walk without a deck tilting beneath his feet.

Fionna looked about ready to weep with relief as she led her horse off the livestock ship and onto the docks of Ayr. She had lost significant weight from her already thin frame.

"We need to fatten you up," Galahad had remarked, falling into step beside her.

"Your lips to the goddess's ears," Fionna murmured. "Give me another ten minutes and I'll be so hungry I could eat a whole cow in one sitting."

Galahad chuckled to himself at the memory before reaching into his saddlebag. His fingers searched around for something, anything, and made contact with a strip of dried venison. He had only two strips left, the only food stores he possessed untouched by the finger of death and rot in this goddess-forsaken land. Steering his horse beside Fionna's, he reached out and gently pressed the dried venison into her cold-stiffened fingers. "Until you get a whole cow to eat in one sitting." They were out of rations after the voyage. Though they had restocked in Ayr, the foul—almost preternatural—weather quickly spoiled most of their newly gathered supplies. They would need to find provisions in Castellum Puellarum—and desperately—before embarking to Caer Benic. Galahad was lucky he had even scrounged up this piece.

"Thank ye," Fionna smiled sleepily, as though the act took the energy of a full day's practice on the tourney round. And then she woodenly nibbled a tiny bite between her front teeth.

Galahad swung his gaze up ahead onto the narrow trail for a glimpse of the emerging village beneath the dormant volcano of Castle Rock.

High on a hill above them, just visible through the sheet of white, a ghostly timber and stone fortress dominated the landscape, like something made by Odin himself. Winding, compacted-earth streets snaked up the hill throughout the tidy turf-sided buildings. They had made it. But Castellum Puellarum was not what he had expected. Even the name differed here. A post outside of the village read "Eiden's Burgh"—Anglo-Saxon rather than Roman. From the stories that had reached his ears from his time as a squire, he expected a large, bustling city. But there was not a soul in sight.

Arthur pulled Llamrei to a stop next to Galahad, surveying the village, a troubled look on his face. "It's so quiet."

"Where is everyone?" Percival asked. "When I came here with my father as a wee lad, these streets were full to the brim."

"Is it still early?" Fionna asked, her voice slurred and drowsy. "I've lost all sense of time."

Galahad frowned as an uneasy feeling twisted his stomach. "Just past mid-day. There should be fishermen stringing up their early morning catch, people tending to their gardens . . ." His voice trailed off as he spotted a couple of small croft plots, now barren.

"Perhaps there's a festival, drawing people into the village center?" Fionna murmured weakly. But Galahad could tell by the tight set of her jaw that even she didn't believe her own words.

"Or perhaps, there's foul magic afoot," Lancelot said. "Could this be Morgana's doing?"

"My half-sister dogs our journey," Arthur replied, his voice hesitant. "But I'm not sure even she is capable of making the people within an entire village disappear." Arthur squared his shoulders. "Whatever is going on here, this changes nothing. We need provisions and then we need to find our way to Caer Benic. Percival, I think this would be a good time to keep the adder stone handy. Everyone else, swords at the ready. I agree with Lancelot. Something strange has bewitched Eiden's Burgh. We must be on alert."

The knights rode up the narrow streets single file, their swords out, save Fionna. She was still too weak and her body slumped slightly, as if talking had consumed what remained of her strength.

A thick, wet fog mixed with the bluish mist, blanketing the buildings and glistening along thatched roofs. Haar or sea fret, if Galahad remembered the term correctly. The kind of sea mist that clung to fur and eyelashes and seeped cold fingers into a man's bones until he rattled and his teeth chattered hard enough to fall out. A different kind of cruel cold than the mist they had traveled through for days.

Though the hour had reached mid-day, an oppressive gray sky hung low overhead. They saw not a single soul in the houses or shops they passed by, nor on the street. Not even a rat scurrying in the gutter or a bird soaring overhead. Had a vile plague darkened their doors? Though, the smell of death didn't linger in the air.

The knights remained as silent as the ghostly village around them. Somehow, speaking seemed wrong, even if a hushed whisper. Galahad had experienced magic before, even black magic, like Morgana and her sisters' curse on Caerleon. But this . . . this was something altogether different. This was Otherworldly.

When Fionna broke the silence, her warbled words were deafening. "Should we check that inn for food?" She pointed to a nearby longhouse with a sign dangling from the roof's beam: "The Glæd Bard."

Lancelot cocked his head. "I do not speak barbarian." He looked at Galahad, a faint smirk playing on his lips. "Translate?"

"Anglo-Saxon for 'happy.'" Galahad smirked back at Lancelot, refusing to give in to the man's jibe.

"I doubt crabapple is feeling verra jolly right now," Percival muttered under his breath, completely unaware of Galahad and Lancelot's silent poke at one another. But Galahad couldn't help but grin at their mopey, dark knight as the last word left Percival's mouth.

"I bet you're right, Percy," Galahad said. "He probably doesn't even know the meaning of the word."

Lancelot rolled his eyes.

Galahad dismounted first and assisted Fionna while Percival tied up their horses.

The inside of the inn's common room was even more eerie. Tables and benches sat neatly throughout the room, and a row of clay pitchers lined the wall behind a large serving table, beside stacks of oak barrels. But the center fire pit and candles were dark. And the place was completely empty.

"What happened to all the people?" Arthur asked, seemingly to no one.

"Everything is neat, just as they left it," Lancelot said. "A raid hasn't killed or driven off the townsfolk. This is magic."

"Percival, do you see anything strange?" Arthur asked.

Percival shook his head, drawing his cloak tighter around himself. "Nae. Everything appears . . . as though a macabre tapestry."

Fionna's stomach rumbled audibly. She pressed her hands to her midsection, as if to keep her hunger quiet. "Perhaps we could see if they left anything to eat?"

"I'm feeling quite peckish myself," Galahad said. "I'm sure even this empty village of ghouls will look better after a good meal and a fire."

Without another word, the knights settled Fionna into a chair and then dispersed through the inn, into every alcove and walled-off space, poking about every cooking utensil.

Percival stood up from where he had been peering into a storage chest with a look of dismay. "Empty."

Lancelot and Arthur appeared out of a back room. "The pots and barrels are empty," Arthur said, almost apologetically at Fionna. "Not a crumb."

Galahad nodded, holding up a log. "I found nothing but firewood."

"Water?" Arthur asked.

"Perhaps in a nearby well," Lancelot suggested.

"All right," Arthur said. "We're going to bed down here for the night. Percival and Lancelot, get the horses set up properly and see if there's water to boil. Galahad, make us the biggest fire you can manage. Fionna, your job is to eat every scrap bit of food we can rummage from our saddlebags."

"But—" she began to protest, but Arthur held up a hand.

"You haven't had a full meal in a week. The rest of us will live. You *need* to eat."

Her stomach rumbled again, and she nodded.

Interlude

Morgana

Perched on a window ledge, the crow angled her head to track the mortals with her beady eye. She could see the spectral ribbons of fears dancing wildly before their vision, those same threads building cobwebs in their minds.

Swords half-drawn, the males circled around the witch, who appeared sickly and weak. The crow almost cawed in laughter. They were more skittish than a field mouse scurrying away from an owl. But then the large male with golden hair strode by the window and gained her attention. His deep voice rumbled even the fog blanketing the *In-Between*. Then another voice, one more familiar, pierced through the shadows and illusions.

Him.

The male with tumbling darkness for hair and the Otherworld's veiled mist for eyes. He belonged to her. He was *her* possession, not the Little Dragon King's. And certainly not the witch's or the other male's, the one with magic in his blood. Unable to resist the lure of his scent, the call of his voice, the crow fluttered to the ground and transformed.

Morgana crept to the sill and peered inside from the shadows. The magic of the *In-Between* made her invisible until she granted the powers here permission to help her fully materialize. Still, she used caution, not wishing to disturb the trap.

She could see, even now, the mortals' unease. The landscape around them unsettled them in its emptiness and quiet. How little they understood the Otherworld was laughable. Not even the witch or the Fisher whelp, who had magic singing in their blood, possessed The Sight. Rather, they saw only darkness and space, uncomprehending how the bone key they carried had allowed them to pass through the mortal realm and into the *In-Between*—the thin veil between the human world and the faerie Otherworld—where even more dangerous monsters tread.

True, the key would unlock the gate to Caer Benic and their precious Grail. But it also unlocked other doors. And so, earlier in the week, while the party traversed Strathclyde, she had used the morning's fog to weave with the *In-Between*'s mist to funnel them into the hushed shadows of this place. Conjuration was magic she particularly enjoyed—perfect for implanting ideas in dreams or to terrorize through nightmares. Or to lure warriors to their deaths through visions of a beautiful maiden. Perhaps one by a streamside, collecting berries. The red stains on her lips the blood she thirsts to drink from their veins as they lay dying.

And lure a warrior she would. Fogging the

window with her breath, she wrote runes onto the glass. As her fingertip formed the last line, Lancelot snapped his intense gaze to where she stood. But he couldn't see her. Rather, he would feel a longing to peer out the window and search for whom his heart desired. Slowly, he ambled across the creaking floor to the fogged glass and cupped his eyes to peer outside, looking right through her.

Morgana traced the outline of his face with her finger. "You do not belong here, prince," she whispered to each beloved, cursed feature. "You are of no value to this quest. Forsake my brother and his witch and I will forgive you. Together, as a mortal son from the Isle of Man and a fae daughter from the Otherworld, we will reign this wretched land. The people will finally accept you. Finally *love* you."

Lancelot stepped back from the window, his dark brows furrowed, his beautiful lips tipped down in a frown. With a sigh, long and slow, he twisted away from her and moved beside the fire, his shoulders slumped.

Cackling with delighted laughter, Morgana's body faded into the swirling fog until she was born aloft by the unnatural wind. The crow glided across the false city of Castellum Puellarum to the *In-Between*'s Castle of the Maidens. Time to alert her sisters and fellow sídhe priestesses that their guests were soon to arrive.

Chapter Twenty

Fionna

I shivered under the thin blankets, praying for sleep. We had used up all the firewood we could find in the common room, but none of us had wanted to brave the rain or the unsettling quiet of the city to venture out and look for more. So, the center fire pit was now dark and cold.

I had experienced worse, I reminded myself as I tried to unclench my frigid muscles enough to let sleep take me. One fighting season, when cattle raids were especially bad, the snow had come early. With nowhere to properly hide, I had slept under the boughs of an oak tree with only my cloak above me and a fellow fiann mate at my back. I worried endlessly about losing fingers and toes those two days, rubbing my limbs and digits regularly. The cold hard bed below me now was luxury compared to that near misadventure. Grasping at gratitude, I finally drifted to sleep.

But my sleep was as restless and as troubled as the hours leading up to the moment we huddled up for the night. I found myself back on the Scarlet Selkie, the swaying and undulating of the sea stealing my equilibrium and my dignity once more. The sky above the dream state Welsh longboat was roiling with storm clouds. A streak of lightning danced across the sky, followed by a crack of bellowing thunder. I stood and ducked out from beneath the protective burlap cloth. The rain slashed against my face, plastering my hair to my scalp. But I was alone. The crew, the captain, Arthur and the other knights, they were nowhere to be found. The sails cracked wildly in the wind, ropes like thrashing snakes twisting against my feet. I ran for a set of oars near the stern, plunging the paddles into the swirling ocean, trying to slow the ship's wild movement. But I couldn't. As lightning split the sky, whitening the deadly sea in my vision momentarily, my breath caught in my throat. A wave stood before me, tall as Arthur's keep, impossible to avoid. I dove for the mast, wrapping my arms around the solid oak post. Clinging to the wood and ropes with all my strength. But when the wave hit me, the momentum was too powerful. The water hit with the force of a hundred tonnes, ripping my fingers from the mast and tossing me into the frigid, uncaring sea. Up was down, right was left. I fell into darkness. My chest screaming for air.

I bolted upright, my lungs gasping, as if they had truly been straining for their last breath. In the still blackness, my hand strayed to my forehead, where clammy sweat beaded on my brow. Ten frantic heartbeats passed before my eyes adjusted to the darkness and I realized where I was. No longer was I in Eiden's Burgh. I was back home. In Aghanravel. I was in the bed that I shared with Aideen. I threw off the covers and biting cold air gnashed at the exposed skin of my face, neck, and hands.

"Father? Aideen?" I called out, my mind struggling to make sense.

How had I returned here? What in the hell was going on? I threw open the front door and ran into a hazy dawn. The landscape looked like my home. The crooked, wattle fence post, the trough for the horses and pigs, the little stretch of garden beneath the eaves that Aideen tended to daily. But everything was wrong.

The lush land surrounding my father's home was barren—blackened like the black of the rivers in Caerleon. The tall birch trees were stark, bare skeletons, Aideen's garden shriveled and dead. *What happened here?* I turned slowly in a circle, horror permeating every fiber of my body. *Not here too.* How had Morgana known? Was this the work of the fae? Had Aghanravel been torched? But no—the house was untouched.

I saw a figure in the distance with chestnut hair flowing in the wind, a dress of cornflower blue and gray wrapped onto her thin frame. "Aideen?" I cried out, excitement warring with alarm within me. I took a few tentative steps toward her and then broke into a run, flying at my sister. "Aideen!"

I spun her around. But when I saw her face, a ragged gasp broke from me. I recoiled, a sob prickling the back of my throat. Aideen's eyes were lifeless, her skin a patchwork of black spiderwebs. The curse . . . the dark magic had taken her too. I caressed Aideen's hair, her arms, taking her face between my hands.

"Aideen. Wake up, *mo chroí*. Fight the curse. I'll find a way to fix this. I'll find a way to heal you."

Aideen opened her mouth to say something.

Relief welled in me. My sister was still in there somewhere.

"Yes, Aideen?" I asked.

But out of my sister's mouth came a singular sound. Foreign and grating.

The single caw of a crow.

I jerked awake, tangled in my blankets. I was in the inn in Eiden's Burgh. I flopped back into my bed, trying to slow my racing heartbeat. Goddess above, they had only been dreams. Horrible, horrible dreams. I threw off the tangle of blankets, moving toward a window, trying to gather my wits about me. The rain had let up and was now just a misty drizzle on the windowpanes. The night was still dark though. Unnaturally so.

I heard a caw in the distance and whirled toward the source, my eyes going wide. Was the bird inside the inn?

Grabbing my sword, I tip-toed back toward our circle around the fire pit, searching for Arthur in the dark. I didn't want to wake him, if I were going mad. Arthur's bedroll was empty. What? Where was he?

I moved quietly to Percival's bedroll. Empty as well.

Galahad's. Empty.

The caw sounded again. I froze. It had emanated

from down the hallway, near the back door. Lancelot's post. I lifted my sword and crept toward the back end of the inn. I rounded a corner, letting my eyes adjust to the dim light inside. I sighed audibly when I saw Lancelot's form curled up within his bedroll.

But my relief was short-lived. Something was wrong. I crept closer and when I saw him—truly—I couldn't stop the garbled scream from escaping my throat.

He lay on the bed, his form limp. His eyes—his eyes . . . "No, no, no!" I cried, pressing against a wall. His eyes had been pecked out.

A deafening caw from behind chilled my blood and I leaped, spinning. A huge crow perched at the window. As soon as my eyes met the beast's, the bird launched from the windowsill and flew out into the rainy night.

I sat up. A sob escaped me. I was in bed—disoriented and terrified. Was this a dream? Another dream within a dream? Or goddess . . . Lancelot . . .

I threw my covers off and ran down the hallway toward where Lancelot lay before the back door. I burst around the corner. "Lancelot!" I crossed the back room in a blink, falling at his side.

He startled awake as my fingers found his face, the soft unbroken skin of his eyelids. I felt across his stubbled jaw, the peaks of his cheekbones, the smooth expanse of his temple. Relief uncoiled within me, my body nearly toppling over limp and spent. He was alive. And he was whole.

"Fionna?" He asked groggily. His voice was low and rasping with sleep. "What's going on?"

"I had a dream," I managed, my fingers still straying over his face of their own volition. "Ye were . . ." embarrassment prickled me as my voice caught in my throat, thick with threatening tears.

"Shhh," he whispered, wrapping an arm around me and pulling me into the crook beneath his shoulder. "It's all right. I'm fine. Gods, woman, you're frigid!" He pulled open the blankets to usher me inside. "Get in here before you die of cold."

I let him wrap me in the comfort of his blankets and his arms, breathing in the scent of mint and moonlight that was all Lancelot. I shivered against him—whether from the cold of the night or my fright at the dream, I wasn't sure. I couldn't get the image out of my mind—the dark bloody wounds where his eyes had once been.

"What happened? You had a bad dream?"

"The images were so real," I said, suddenly feeling like a foolish child, and wanting to explain myself. "I was having another dream, and I woke up in my bed here, but everyone was gone. Everyone but ye. And ye . . . yer eyes had been pecked out. There was a massive crow." My shivers wracked me against the hard muscle of Lancelot's body.

"All is well," he murmured into my hair, pulling me tighter against him. His warmth was beginning to leech into me, to soothe my nerves. "Morgana's shadow hangs over all of us. Especially in this place. I don't know why, but fae magic is strong here. I'm not surprised foul thoughts invaded your dreams. But rest assured, I am alive and whole. I would put up quite a fight before I would allow anyone to peck out my eyes."

"And quite a racket?" I asked, cracking a small smile. I imagined muttered curses and crashing about, if Lancelot truly went to battle with a giant crow inside the tiny end room of this inn.

"I'll make a huge racket. There would be no way you could sleep through my annoyance."

"Promise?" I asked, looking up at him in the dark. My eyes drank in the sight of him so close—the tangle of his hair, the smooth expanse of his skin beneath me. My hands itched to rove freely over the muscles of his chest and shoulders. But I held myself still, not knowing how far our truce extended. Not wanting to ruin this moment.

"I promise, Fi," Lancelot whispered, and gently kissed my brow.

My heart squeezed at the nickname. Fi was what Aideen called me since girlhood. But Fi sounded especially sweet on Lancelot's lips. Thoughts of Aideen sent my stomach churning again—the memory of the horrible dream version of her and the real woman, who was perhaps just as doomed.

"You were so worried," Lancelot looked down at me, his light eyes shining in the dark. "When you feared me dead . . ." he trailed off. His words were tentative, as if he couldn't quite dare believe. Fool man. Of course, I cared for him!

"Does it truly surprise ye that the thought of finding ye wounded and bleeding terrifies me? Did I not make clear to ye after Twrch Trwyth that I would like ye whole and intact?"

"I recall the angry lecture . . . the rest is a little

blurry. I could use a refresher."

I snorted. "Oh, could ye? Well let me put it more plainly, Lancelot du Luc. I want ye alive. The only way ye're dying is if I stab ye myself, ye infuriating goat."

Lancelot softly laughed. "Consider the feeling mutual." He tucked a stray braid behind my ear, gazing down at me. His look unarmed me. There was a raw tenderness there I had never seen until this moment. How could he hide his vulnerability so well?

"I care for ye, Lancelot," I whispered as I traced the curved shell of his ear. "And I always will."

Lancelot closed his eyes briefly, shuddering under my ministrations. And when they fluttered back open, the glinting steel of his eyes were alight with a fire. A cool heat that thrilled me deep down to my core. He seized my arms and then rolled me beneath him in one swift movement, the shock of the cold air mingling with the heat of his lips on mine.

Chapter Twenty-One

Lancelot

Fionna's kiss was the most bewitching sensation Lancelot had ever known. Her touch a magic unparalleled. A hot chill stole its way down his spine, igniting every dark and lonely corner of his soul. His heart drank greedily, desperately. To him, there was nothing more alluring than a woman who asserted herself—confident and comfortable with her own body. With her own mind.

Fionna's tongue thrust between his lips and his chest heaved with desire. *Claim me*, he wanted to shout. *Make me yours.* Lancelot had little fight left in him and he yielded to the warrior's body pressed firmly to his. A warrior who was his equal.

"Fi . . ." Lancelot pulled away just far enough for his breath to tangle with hers. He cupped her face and whispered, "I want to know your . . . love."

"Then allow me to love ye."

Those words unlocked a hidden flood of grief within him. A gnawing hunger took over—a desperate need to be loved, to be wanted, dousing all reason within him.

With practiced grace, Lancelot rolled Fionna over to top him. Whispered warnings clamored in his racing mind. But when she fisted his tunic and yanked him up to meet her lips, the whispers silenced. His heartbeat knew only hers.

Lancelot, now sitting up, gripped her hips and positioned her across his lap.

Fionna's legs curled around his lower back, her fingers tracing the indigo knots and swirls peeking out from his tunic. Then she leaned forward and her tongue flicked out, to lick along the lines of his tattoos.

He groaned softly, his head falling back. A breath fluttered free from his chest. *More.* He needed *more.*

Their lips collided in a thrilling rush, a wildness breaking through their carefully built walls. She clawed at his back, her nails raking his skin even through the wool tunic. Narrow hips and flexing stomach muscle ground into his, her rhythm fast and urgent. His hands roamed the expanse of her shoulders, her arms, wanting to feel the flex and pull of her strength. Wanting to know both her softness and hardness simultaneously. And her fight. Gods, her fight. He snaked his hands up her back, until his fingers grasped her braids and yanked her head back. A wicked smile played across her swollen lips. Skies above, she would ruin any lingering self-control he possessed.

Skin, as breathtaking as a first snow, called to him. Her neck lay bared to the night, the same expanse he had once held a sword to. The memory shuddered through him. His foolishness. His anger. As he lowered his lips to her submissive stretch of skin, he breathed deeply her scent of heathered moors, of moss-covered rocks, and the biting cold of a Northern sea breeze. His tongue flicked out and tasted her sweetness first before he scraped the edge of his teeth along the tender skin.

Fionna moaned, and his cock hardened tight at her pleasure. And so, he bit her—hard—where her shoulder met her neck.

"Lance . . ." she breathed, deepening the grind of her hips, the tight grip of her fist in his tunic. The sound twisted his heart until he bled out, his treacherous organ aching to die in her arms. But a thought battled against his arousal, a thought that blazed hot as a refining fire. The only person who ever called him Lance was Arthur.

Arthur.

Lancelot wrenched back, shoving himself out of her embrace. "Gods, I'm a bloody idiot!"

Fionna fell on her arse and gaped at him, shock and hurt glittering in her silver eyes. A gaze he could perfectly see from the sliver of moonlight breaking through the storm clouds and fog outside.

"Done with me already, are ye?"

"No, nothing like that." Lancelot huffed out an irritated breath and a dark curl floated away from his eyes. "I . . . I can't . . . this . . . goddess save me." He stood and began pacing the short stretch of the hallway, back and forth. His pulse galloped loud in his ears. His breath came quick and hard, almost matching the shaking in his hands. In a moment of weakness, he had almost unleashed another curse on Arthur, on Caerleon. "Sorry," he muttered before turning his back to her.

"Sorry?" she spat. "I'm not some trifling maiden to conquest and discard." Lancelot winced, a muscle pulsing in his clenched jaw. Fionna shuffled to her feet behind him and then grabbed his arm, spinning him toward her. "Nor is my body available for whenever the mood fancies yer famous cock."

He remained silent, his gaze unyielding.

"Do ye still love her?"

"Morgana?" Lancelot reared back, as if slapped. "Hell no."

"Is there something wrong with me, then?"

Lancelot relaxed his body further into an aloof posture and derisively said one word—the one he knew would seal his betrayal in her mind. But would save Arthur.

"Yes."

Fionna stumbled back a step. The pain in her gaze ripped through him, but he remained steady, staring her down. The angrier she was with him, the better. For everyone.

"I don't believe ye, Lancelot du Lac. Ye wanted me, *begged* to know my love." Fionna stepped into his space and pushed on his shoulder with two, strong fingers. "Fight me until yer last breath, but I will still care for ye, no matter what. But do *not* touch me again until yer sure of yer heart."

She swiveled on her heel, hair whipping through the shadows, before fading down the hallway and into the nightmare that had become his life.

When he was certain she was gone, he breathed again. But it hurt—to breathe. Every draw of air ached hot between his ribs. Every exhale chilled his tattered soul.

Lancelot fell to his knees and buried his face into his hands, slowly lowering his forehead to the bitter cold floor. The icy shock on his skin rippled through him. His body began to shake, but not from the un-natural wintered air or the frozen floors. Tears, long buried, surfaced with a vengeance. A sob loosened in his chest as his heart continued to bleed out.

It would kill him anew each time he rejected Fionna's gift of love. A love he had desperately want-ed to know for so long. Every day he would have to hold himself apart, to be cruel to her—the most mag-nificent woman he had ever known. He was useless to Arthur now, to his sword-brothers, to himself.

Perhaps he should have just given his head to Morgana. Perhaps they would all be better off with-out him.

Chapter Twenty-Two

Arthur

Arthur peered through the window. The storm from last night had moved on, leaving only the Haar fog that had greeted them when first arriving in this cursed place. His eyes narrowed as he caught sight of something. Craning his neck, he moved closer, squinting his eyes at the foreboding fortress high on the hill above them.

Was that? . . . It was! A light in the castle window.

Excitement surged Arthur's pulse into a gallop. Light meant people. And people meant food. And perhaps an explanation for the madness behind this ghostly village.

Arthur woke Galahad, Percival, and Lancelot quickly, and they rose without much complaint. Though, it was evident that a good night's sleep had also eluded his sword-brothers.

He paused before Fionna's bedroll, inhaling a breath. When he knelt beside her, the splay of her white braids across the pillow seized his heart. A sight he wanted to wake to each morning.

Lost to his fevered thoughts, he bent over her to softly press a kiss to her cheek, forgetting about the knights behind him. But then he froze, his animal instincts kicking in and snapping him back to reality. Something cold and sharp nicked his neck.

Her eyes were wild, her teeth bared. A dagger was clutched in her fist, the naked blade held steady against his exposed throat.

"Arthur," she breathed, and then her hand dropped as the confusion in her face cleared.

"Remind me not to surprise you in bed," Arthur joked as he straightened. His hand strayed to his throat and his fingers came away with a tiny drop of blood.

"Waking to yer face each morning would be a welcome surprise," she said, standing. "If not for this place, that is. Eiden's Burgh sets me on edge."

Fionna's words warmed him and he fought a creeping flush. "You're not the only one," he said. "I want to be gone from here as quickly as I can."

She pulled on her boots and then trailed Arthur to where the other knights were gathering their saddlebags and donning cloaks. Dark shadows lined their faces, as if the cold and hunger of last night had aged them beyond their years.

"I saw a light in the castle," Arthur announced. "I think we should investigate before we leave the village."

"A light could mean people," Galahad said.

"Could mean food," Percival added.

"My thoughts exactly." Arthur nodded.

"Aye, what are we waiting fer?" Percival asked.

The knights quickly saddled their horses and set off into the empty streets.

Arthur had visited Castellum Puellarum once before, when he was a boy. He remembered how impressive the keep had seemed—what a feat of engineering and construction—how many men and beasts it must have taken to get those stones so high upon the hill. He was struck by a similar sense of awe today, but the wonder warred with the trepidation this empty village stirred within him. He prayed the castle would provide much-needed answers.

They remained silent until they finally summited the high hill. Though worry etched lines into each face, it seemed like no one wanted to express their hesitation.

They rode through the castle's gaping front gates to find a courtyard as lifeless as everything else in Eiden's Burgh.

"Perhaps they're inside?" Percival finally asked. The absence of his kinsmen had seemed to dim even Percival's unflappable good mood.

"Perhaps," Arthur concurred. Despite the light he had seen, he knew not what they would find within the castle walls.

Inside the huge oaken front door, the fortress resembled the village. Empty hallways furnished for invisible inhabitants. But the air inside the castle was warmer and grew even warmer the farther they walked.

"Do I feel a hearth fire?" Fionna asked, her face lifted to the shadows as though the very sun.

They were towed down the hallway by the blissful heat, the walls they passed ornamented with dark tapestries and crossed swords and impressive antlers.

"In here," Percival said, turning a corner.

Percival was right. Around the corner, two open doors welcomed their party. Light and heat emanated from inside.

Arthur held his breath, not sure of what to expect, for nothing here was as it should be. But here—here was an even bigger surprise.

Percival laughed in delight, and Fionna clapped her hands over her mouth.

"I think I'm dreaming," she said.

"I'm in the same dream," Lancelot agreed. "Because I see a feast before me, set for a king."

"Well, we have a king here. Two if ye count me," Percival said with a sly smirk at Arthur. "So, let's feast!"

The room was warm and cheerful and brightly lit. Sconces flickered on the wall, candelabras graced each table, and a wooden chandelier spilled amber light from above. Near the banquet, two half-wall hearths roared merrily ablaze. And set before them on a table, as long as a jousting tiltyard, was a cornucopia unlike anything Arthur had ever seen.

Glistening roast quail and duck; crisp, lovely apples as green as a spring field; loaves of bread, fresh and warm. Pies—of what type he didn't know—but with crusts so flakey, his mouth watered as he imagined each bite melting on his tongue. The smells wafted together in a heady perfume—warm spices and cool mint and the yeasty smell of fresh bread.

"Is that—" Fionna began to ask, gravitating toward the table, her eyes wide. "This can't be!" She retrieved a sliced pastry reverently, turning the morsel toward them. "These are like the caraway seed cake Aideen makes." And without another word, she bit into the dessert, her eyes fluttering closed. "Ohmuhgahddess," she murmured around a full bite. She swallowed thickly. "Perhaps sacrilege to say, but I think this caraway seed cake is even better than Aideen's."

Percival floated toward the table, too, his fingers snagging a glistening sausage. "They made these cured meats back home," he said and took a bite, the juice dripping down his chin. His eyes closed as he shuddered in delight. "Lamb, just as I remembered . . ."

Arthur found his feet moving. There were drinks calling to him—pitchers of ale so cold condensation dripped down the side—a rare treat—plus a half-dozen carafes of sweet wine. He picked up a pomegranate, and he could feel his mouth soften into a sad smile. "My mother used to feed these to me when I was a child," Arthur said. "I always felt like a little heathen with the red juice all over my fingers."

"What a beautiful fruit," Fionna said, tilting her head in wonder.

"And delicious," Lancelot added. "I remember those. Traders would bring pomegranates to our shores with tales of a new god from the East."

"How is this possible?" Arthur asked.

Fionna polished off the pastry with a last bite. "I am too hungry to care. Are not ye?"

Galahad was the only one hanging back, Arthur noticed, his knight's face grave. "Something is wrong. This smells of magic."

"Nae, it smells of minced meat pie!" Percival had retrieved a slice of pie and was biting into the dense fruited filling.

"Lancelot?" Galahad asked. "Think of the faerie wine Morgana sent us. This could be a trap, don't you think?"

"I tend to agree," Lancelot said. "But, Fionna and Percival have already eaten. Do you feel anything?"

"I feel like I'm going to eat someone's arm off, if they don't let me eat this food," Fionna snapped, picking up a cluster of grapes and popping one into her mouth.

"I don't feel any different," Percival said. "Except fuller than I've been in days."

"Perhaps this was left for us by someone who is on our side," Arthur said. "Like the standing stones and faerie-scribed plaque. Not all magic has harmed us. We desired food, did we not? This may very well be a gift that we shouldn't squander."

"Ye're a smart man, Yer Majesty," Percival said, pointing a caramelized duck leg at him with a hasty bow before taking a large bite. He still held a half-eaten pie in the other hand.

"What about the adder stone," Galahad suggested. "Perhaps the talisman will reveal a warning?"

Percival gestured toward the pocket of his tunic with his head, raising his pie and duck leg. "Grab it, ye fussy old woman."

"Fool Scot," Galahad grumbled, but crossed to

Percival and riffled around in his pocket, seizing the stone.

"That tickles," Percival laughed, and Galahad mock cuffed him.

"Anything?" Arthur asked.

Galahad surveyed the table from one end to the other. "I don't see any sign of enchantment. The food looks . . . normal."

"Thank the gods," Lancelot said, falling upon a dripping slice of roast beef like a dying man while pouring himself a goblet of wine.

Arthur pulled up a chair, retrieving a silver trencher, and then carefully began to select perfectly prepared food from various platters and bowls.

Galahad frowned, shaking his head. "Still doesn't feel right. If this food isn't enchanted, then servants should be bustling about. Where are they? Why did their Lord abandon this feast?"

The questions swirled in Arthur's mind, filling him with disquiet. Galahad was right. Something was going on here that baffled the mind. But, if they were to solve this mystery, at least they could do so on a full stomach. So, he took a bite.

Chapter Twenty-Three

Fionna

I leaned back in a pleasant haze. My belly was taut with the delicious meal, my head buzzing with the heady wine I had guzzled. I had eaten my fill, my stomach blessedly cooperating for the first time since leaving Wales.

Percival sat in a chair beside me. Lancelot watched below lowered lashes, I noticed, as their cheerful knight, with drooping eyelids, licked the sticky sugar off his fingers from his third pear tart. "Och, I've never had such wonderful fare." Percival patted his belly happily, pouring himself another goblet of wine.

"Galahad, any luck?" Arthur asked drowsily from the head of the table, before he downed the dregs from his jug of ale.

Galahad prowled the far edge of the long room, his fists clenching and unclenching at his sides. "Nothing. Not hide nor hair of whoever cooked this feast, nor even scraps of ingredients. The food is magic, I'm telling you."

"The only magic I feel is the delightful headiness of wine," I said, pouring myself another goblet full. "Nothing more, nothing less."

While the rest of us gorged ourselves, Galahad had refused to eat even the tiniest crumb. I frowned, remembering the sparse provisions he had shared with me the night before. His longing for the food was plain, and his stomach grumbled noisily several times. The poor man had to be beyond starving at this point. Perhaps the delusions of hunger had altered his good sense. Instead of partaking among his friends, he stormed from the room to explore the castle, vowing to discover every secret. Seemed like the secrets had eluded him, though.

"We aren't disputing that magic could be at work here," Lancelot said.

He waggled his fingers toward the wine nestled near me, and I passed the pitcher over.

"What the charming prince said." Percival gave Lancelot an official-looking head nod. "We just don't care at this particular moment." He then released an appreciative belch. "'Scuse me," he added, looking at me apologetically.

Like I hadn't heard ten times worse living with my fiann. I let loose a belch of my own, even louder than Percival's. All the knights' heads swiveled my way, their eyes wide with shock.

"Princess Fionnabhair Allán!" Arthur whistled appreciatively as I started to laugh. The wine was filling me with a drowsy warmth and silliness I hadn't felt in so long.

"My father only had girls," I gushed out. "But he

raised me to be his heir. So, naturally, I had to hold my own with the boys. I could drink any of ye under the table." I wiggled my eyebrows at them.

"That sounds like a challenge, My Lady," Lancelot leaned forward, a wicked gleam in his eye and a flirty smile on his lips.

"Even Galahad?" Percival arched a copper brow. "He drinks as much as a war horse. Don't ye, chipmunk?"

"Our dear Galahji . . ." I tried to say his full Norse name but garbled each foreign sound terribly as my tongue tripped over itself.

"I'll go under the table with ye," Percival said to me with a rascally grin and a wink.

I snorted with laughter as I continued. "Our Gally has been replaced by a boring, serious old man." I lowered my voice to sound like Galahad and said, "I am Galahad the Gallant." The knights all burst into laughter, encouraging me on. "For fun, I like to wear the color green, skip across meadows, and ruin my friends' happiness at finally filling their empty bellies."

Galahad glowered at me from his position by the far fireplace, ignoring our laughter. "Someone has to keep you fools from getting harmed. Or am I the only one who remembers the incident with the faerie wine?"

Memories of the night with the faerie wine heated my blood as images flashed by my mind's eye—of Arthur's passionate kiss, Galahad's sultry moves, and Percival's grip on my hips. I wouldn't mind a repeat of Alworn's enchanted vintage just now. Need coiled deep within me, low and hot, as my eyes flitted from Lancelot to Percival to Arthur. I wasn't sure what I wanted in this moment—who I wanted—only that going to bed alone would be an unnecessary shame.

"You've had enough." Galahad strode across the room to the table, prying the goblet from my fingers gently but firmly. "Bed is in order."

The others protested, their words twining together.

"Now see here—" Arthur began.

"—what makes you—" Lancelot pushed to his feet unsteadily.

"Let the lady stay!" Percival protested.

"All of you fools are going to bed," Galahad snapped, the dark blue of his eyes roiling like a furious sea. "I will be depositing Fionna in a room where she can sleep off this wine. *Alone*." The threat in his tone seemed to mollify the others.

"Oh fine." Arthur heaved a sigh. "A good night's sleep would do us all good. We have a long journey in the morning." He stood and then leaned heavily against the table. I hadn't seen Arthur this relaxed in so long. Perhaps ever. And now I truly didn't want the night to end.

I pouted, shoving against Galahad's bulk. I might as well as have tried to pull a great oak from the ground by its tangled roots. Completely useless.

The world tilted beneath me wonderfully, all heady, every sensation a swirling wave of bliss. Several giddy heartbeats later, I registered that Galahad had picked me up in his arms, as easily as a child. "Put me down," I said. "I'm not a hapless maiden!"

But my head lolled against his strong shoulder even as I spoke, dizziness overtaking me once more. Had I drank so much? Apparently I had.

"I found rooms for us," Galahad said, peering over his shoulder.

Through drooping eyes, I watched as Lancelot plopped into his seat, leaning back with his boots atop the table, while Arthur poured himself another drink. Percival had retrieved a fourth pastry and was chewing with a look of rapture softening his face, his eyes closed.

"Now you animals!" Galahad barked, and Arthur, Percival, and Lancelot jumped to their feet guiltily, staggering along behind him toward the hallway.

"Fionna," Percival murmured, stumbling behind Galahad.

"Mmm?" I replied, tilting my head back over Galahad's meaty bicep to survey Percival upside down.

"I need to let ye down easy, lass. This tart has claimed my heart, and there's no room for another, ye ken?"

Lancelot snorted and then broke into hysterical laughter. "A fine wedding, if ever there was one. Huzzah!" He tripped, halfway falling onto the stairway Galahad was now climbing. I had never heard such a genuine laugh from Lancelot. And such a glorious sound it was.

"Think we'll offend your fair bride by eating the rest of her brethren at the reception?" Arthur asked, laughter sputtering through pressed lips as he hauled Lancelot up by his armpits.

"Surrounded by drunken idiots," Galahad grumbled to himself as he summited the stairs.

"Oh Galahad . . ." I murmured to him, stroking his beard as though petting a loyal hound. "No need to be so serious."

"Silly me," he said. "What's so serious about a deadly quest to find an ancient faerie artifact to end a devastating plague now destroying our land?"

I stuck my tongue out at him and then blew out a crude noise.

Arthur, Lancelot, and Percival roared with laughter—Percival stumbling against the wall, holding his stomach and gasping for breath. Lancelot bumped into him and they tangled together, their eyes locked. A current of something powerful passed between them, and I bit back a smile. Crabapple and eternal sunshine? I started to giggle when Lancelot leaned down and affixed his mouth firmly to Percival's.

Arthur's eyebrows shot up before a grin stretched across his face.

"To make your tart jealous," Lancelot murmured as he pushed off the wall, winking at Percival before continuing up the stairs.

Percival watched Lancelot, a silly smile on his blushing face.

I snorted, which caused the knights to erupt into laughter once more.

"Gods help me," Galahad said with a groan as he kicked open a door. "Arthur, Lancelot. This suite of rooms is yours."

I squirmed in his arms as he crossed the hallway and kicked open another door. "Percival. You and I will take this one." While balancing my weight, he shoved Percival inside and pointed at him—"Stay!"

Galahad walked farther down the hall and opened a third door. A dark chamber lay inside, surrounding a large bed cast in shadows. He lay me down gently upon the coverlet. "Rest, Fionna," he said, trying to stand.

But I didn't want to rest. My body was alive with sensation, my blood surging through my veins. I locked my hands around his neck and pulled him back down to me, locking his lips with mine.

My kiss met an impenetrable wall—Galahad's lips were pressed firmly together, unwilling to be swayed by my own. "Fionnabhair—" he said, trying to extricate himself from my ensnaring arms.

"Stay," I pleaded, trying a new tactic by pressing kisses across his jaw line, then up and around the curve of his ear. I snaked my tongue deftly against his earlobe and I felt him shiver above me. Now we were getting somewhere.

"My Lady, no," Galahad snapped. He pried my hands apart, twisting them up above my head where he pressed them into the pillow above me. I struggled briefly against his strong grip, discovering myself well and truly caught. My pulse quickened, and my nipples hardened as desire coursed through me. Perhaps this was a fine tact after all. I surged up to try to capture his mouth with mine, but he shied back.

His handsome face hovered above mine in the dark, his breathing labored. "You are not yourself. If you wish for me tomorrow, I will give you pleasure until the Grail Maiden herself hears you screaming my name all the way from Caer Benic. But tonight, you sleep."

He shoved back from me and crossed the room quickly, closing the door with a decisive click.

I sat up on my elbows, watching the dark door with a pout, before flopping back on the bed with a heavy sigh. How could I sleep? My head was heavy, but my body was alive with desire that flamed through me, the fire pooling insistently between my legs.

Should I go to one of the other knights? I blew out a breath. No, Galahad was right. We needed to sleep. But memories burned bright—the sweet agony of Galahad's length deep within me; Arthur's deft tongue between my legs and his boyish freckles, gods his freckles; Lancelot's weight atop me as his lips spoke what his heart could not; and Percival's hot breath on the crook of my neck as my fingers trailed over his beautiful heart. I squirmed. Perhaps I didn't need a man to reach some satisfaction this night.

My hand was drifting southward when a click sounded across the room—the quiet sound of my door opening. "Who's there?" I looked up, my hand flying to the hilt of my dagger.

"Shh, only me." Arthur's voice reached me as he moved quietly toward the bed.

My heart trilled at the sight of his chiseled jaw, his strong form. His green eyes seemed to flash with preternatural light in the dark. But the thought fled my mind as his weight settled atop me and as his heated lips found mine.

Surely, the flash was merely a trick of moonlight, nothing more.

Chapter Twenty-Four

Galahad

Galahad sagged against the wall outside of Fionna's room, pushing a stray strand of hair from his eyes. By Odin's beard, did the woman have to be so compelling? Did she understand the amount of supernatural strength needed to resist her advances? Yet, he knew he had made the right choice. None of the others were themselves after eating the fare banqueting the large table. To take advantage of her flushed state would have been wrong. No matter how tempting Fionna was, even while intoxicated.

Galahad's empty stomach yowled within him. He was chilled to the marrow of his bones, growing weak from endless hunger, and his balls now ached something fierce. Still, he was strangely proud of himself. As frustrating as the antics were of his king and fellow knights, he was glad to allow them the gift of this night. The curses and Blessed Grail quest consumed their every breath and had for weeks—no, months. Each second was wrapped tight in numerous apprehensions. And these tensions had only grown worse since journeying to Alba. Hearing their genuine laughter, even if summoned forth by an unnatural spell, had done Galahad's heart good. And seeing Lancelot kiss Percival? Well, that was strange. But perhaps not. They would be an interesting pair, if anything moved forward beyond their drunken moment. And less competition for Fionna, that way. That could work in his favor.

His head rolled to the side along the stone wall, and he blinked back images of Fionna in his arms, giggling.

A shadow moved down the hallway toward the staircase they had just summitted.

Galahad froze a single heartbeat before his hand flew to his sword's hilt. He held his breath, his eyes searching in the dark. Slowly, he pulled his sword from its scabbard, the telltale ring of metal-on-metal breaking the corridor's silence.

A flash of white moved quickly, disappearing down the stairs.

"Halt!" Galahad yelled, bolting down the corridor after the apparition. His boots hammered down the stairs until skidding to a stop on the main floor, his head swiveling back and forth wildly as he searched for whoever—or whatever—he had seen.

The hallway remained empty. Torches burned low on the walls and illuminated the space before him. No other soul was here. Galahad's pulse thundered in his ears as he crept forward, sword held aloft. He burst into each room lining the hallway, ready to face whatever beast or man he might find. But each room only held furniture, tapestries, draped windows, and cobwebs. Nothing living.

Toe-to-heel, he prowled into the great hall where the other knights had dined. Panic-stricken shock chilled his blood to ice. The table, heavy-laden with food mere minutes prior, now sat desolate in a room as dark and quiet as the grave. Gone were the dishes, the pitchers of wine and ale, and the roaring hearth that had lured them in from the haar fog.

Galahad whirled around in a circle, his senses firing in alarm. They weren't alone here. Someone was moving. Someone had cleared the feast.

His skin crawled with disquiet as he hurried back up the stairs, sword clutched in his clammy fist. He needed to tell Arthur. They should leave this place. Immediately.

Galahad pushed into the sitting room of Arthur and Lancelot's suite, relieved to find the space empty. He opened the door to the larger of the two attached rooms next, hoping he would find his king within.

"Arth—" Galahad began but stopped. His eyes widened at the vision before him. Then his gaze narrowed in anger. Arthur wasn't alone. His king's muscular back blocked much of the form beneath him, but little imagination was needed to guess whom he entertained. Apparently, Fionna hadn't intended to take no for an answer this night.

Wrapped into each other and oblivious to Galahad's presence, Arthur rolled over in the bed with a satisfied moan. Fionna's white-blonde braids trailed across her bare back as she maneuvered on top of him. Then her body began to move, much as she had moved against Galahad as Percival pleasured her beside him.

He pressed his lips into a thin line, a strange, bleating ache pounding within his heart at the sight. Softly, he let himself out of the room, closing the door behind him. Emotions ignited into a war between his heart and mind, and his hand curled into a fist. Still, as much as he wanted to break up his king and Fionna's coupling out of spite, he wasn't that petty. His brows knitted together. His lips dipping into a frown.

What was he doing? This territorial jealousy wasn't like him. Not really. She could bed and love each of them. Why not? He and Percival were able to share her without ruffled feelings toward one another. And, sharing Fionna with one of his sword-brothers was a pleasure unlike any other—more arousing than he expected. Feeling a bit lighter, Galahad decided he would leave Arthur to his moment and, instead, tell Lancelot and Percival of what he had seen.

Galahad crossed the sitting room and opened the door to the other bedroom, slipping inside. And then sucked in a sharp breath.

No—it wasn't possible. Galahad closed his eyes, rubbing his temple and clearing his thoughts, then snapped his eyes back open. But the vision didn't clear.

In the dim light, Galahad took in the white-blonde of Fionna's braids, the slender curve of her bare waist. She sat astride Lancelot naked as the day she was borne, her hips grinding against Lancelot's in a tantalizing, sensual rhythm as Lancelot's fingers dug into the soft flesh of her arse.

Their moans filled Galahad's ears as he looked uncertainly back at the closed door of Arthur's room. Was *he* going mad? But he hadn't eaten or drank a thing!

Fionna threw back her head with a gasp as Lancelot reached up to cup one perfect breast. The waterfall of her hair fell across her shoulder as she arched, baring her back.

Galahad's breath hitched. His vision narrowed in on her shoulder blades. Her back was far too smooth—no puckered red skin from the healing wound he had stitched up himself. This wasn't Fionna.

The hair on his arms stood on end.

Panic surged through his veins.

He was a humble blacksmith's son and knew not what to do in the face of such strange enchantments. If he confronted this false Fionna, would she turn on him? Would this being hurt Lancelot?

A thought blazed through him as clear and bright as a shooting star. He shoved his hand into his pocket and pulled out the adder stone.

His fingers closed around the talisman, and the shadowy vision before him changed. The white-blonde of Fionna's braids disappeared, along with her familiar form. In her place writhed a curvaceous woman with hair as red as a Beltane fire.

"Get off him!" Galahad surged forward, seizing the faerie by the shoulder and yanking her off Lancelot. She tumbled backwards, but twisted nimbly, coming to her feet with lithe grace. Her exquisite face was twisted in a snarl of rage, her lush lips bared, revealing teeth topped with savage points.

She screamed and leaped at Galahad, moving faster than he would have thought possible. Galahad barely managed to lift his sword in time. But he did—spearing the faerie through her naked abdomen.

"What in the gods' name did you do?!" Lancelot's eyes were wild and unhinged. He leaped off the bed with a growl and then barreled toward Galahad, crashing into him with a powerful fist to Galahad's gut.

"It . . . wasn't . . . her!" Galahad coughed out.

The faerie slid off his sword to crumple on the floor, blood bubbling through her sharp teeth.

Lancelot threw another blow, this time straight at Galahad's head. But Galahad managed to deflect Lancelot's punch with his forearm. He caught his sword-brother's hand in his own, crushing the adder stone into the man's fingers. "Look at her!"

Lancelot did so and then staggered into Galahad. The man blinked, his eyes adjusting in the darkness while his mind was no doubt trying to reconcile what he now saw.

"But—" Lancelot stumbled back, falling to the ground, his hands gripping his tangled hair.

Galahad sagged with relief as Lancelot came back to himself.

"A glamour," Lancelot said as the horror of the situation washed over him.

"Someone is with Arthur," Galahad said, pulling Lancelot to his feet. "I don't know if she's the real Fionna."

"You saved me before our king?" Lancelot grabbed his scabbard and then pulled his sword free, not bothering with clothes. Galahad bit back a sharp reply and followed the infuriating man.

He crossed the sitting room once again and then Galahad opened the door. Lancelot burst in and wrapped one arm around Fionna's waist, pulling her body from Arthur's. And with the adder stone grasped in Galahad's hand, he now saw that she wasn't Fionna. A different faerie had violated their king, this one plump with long golden tresses.

The faerie struggled against Lancelot's grip, shoving free of him as Arthur stood. "Unhand her!" their king barked.

"She's not Fionna," Galahad shouted back, leveling his sword at the sneering creature.

Lancelot did the same.

The faerie tensed to move, her dark eyes flicking between Lancelot and Galahad.

"Stand down!" Arthur cried out, trying to throw an arm across the creature in protection. "Have you two gone frothing mad?"

"Your Majesty, if you have ever trusted me, then listen," Lancelot said, his voice low and hard. "You need to move away from her and toward safety."

"I will not—" Arthur began, but the word was cut off by a garbled cry.

The faerie moved with impossible speed. A spear had materialized in her hand and, in one fluid motion, she had turned on Arthur, stabbing the spearhead into his gut while screaming indecipherable words in the sídhe tongue.

"No!" Lancelot released a war cry and surged forward, stabbing the faerie through the breast with his own blade.

She crumpled backwards, the wicked spear falling from her grip and clattering to the floor. Lancelot stabbed again with another roar of fury, this time driving his sword through the faerie's throat.

She fell still.

Arthur staggered backwards, his hands covering his side where the faerie's weapon had pierced him. A look of incredulity crossed his face as crimson blood seeped through his fingers.

Galahad grabbed the coverlet off the bed as Lancelot helped Arthur sit.

"Easy," Galahad said.

"The others," Arthur coughed. "Fionna is undefended."

"She can hold her own for a moment," Lancelot said as Galahad pressed the bunched cloth to the wound.

"Percival," Arthur coughed. "His vow . . . the Grail . . ."

Galahad and Lancelot looked at each other in horror. If one of these vile faeries successfully seduced Percival, he would lose his connection to the Grail.

The two knights sprang to their feet.

"Go to them," Arthur said, grimacing in pain. And when he saw the hesitation on their face at the prospect of leaving him, he shouted, "That's an order!"

Chapter Twenty-Five

Fionna

My desire for Arthur was an all-consuming blaze, and I was slowly becoming ash beneath his touch. I didn't know if it was the food or the wine or this strange unfamiliar castle, but I found myself unmoored—overcome by the magic that always stirred between us. A connection even more heady with magic this moment. His weight on top of me was an exquisite thrill; his kisses burned hot as fire. I wanted to be destroyed by loving him—to let our passion devour me until we were nothing but skin and moans and soft whispers—no walls, no secrets.

Arthur's freckled face was tucked between my legs, making me writhe in pleasure, when the door to my chamber burst open.

A huge silhouetted form, holding a torch and a sword, appeared in the darkness. And instinct took over to protect my king, pleasure forgotten. I scrambled off the bed for my sword, seizing the hilt and pulling my blade from its scabbard.

But the beast didn't come at me. It went for Arthur, who rolled off the other side of the bed just in time to avoid a deadly sword strike.

I ran at the monster and crashed into its hulking body as it tried to lunge for Arthur once more, knocking the beast sideways off its feet. I fell sideways, too, my own equilibrium unsteady and tilting.

"Fionna!" I heard a familiar voice say.

I sprang back to my feet, sword at the ready, blinking. Then, my eyes came into focus. I knew the huge beast who had invaded my room.

"Galahad?" I asked, stepping back with confusion.

"This isn't Arthur," Galahad shouted, surging toward Arthur, the sharp edge of his sword glinting in the torchlight.

Galahad had gone mad. He was going to kill his king!

"No!" I threw my arms around his huge waist, and my sword tumbled from my grip. With every ounce of strength in my body, I heaved sideways, trying to unbalance Galahad enough to slow him. It worked. We fell sideways into the wall in a thunderous crash. The torch slipped from Galahad's fingers and rolled across the floor where the crackling flame stopped beside a pooled set of curtains. *Oh goddess.*

Flames burst into light with a *whoosh* and then quickly began licking up the woolen curtains.

But I had no time to douse the fire, for Galahad was already leaping to his feet with a cry.

Arthur had taken advantage of our temporary incapacity and was now dashing across the room for the door. But he didn't get far. Another figure appeared in the doorway, blocking his exit.

A sharp breath seized my lungs. Goosebumps fleshed over my body in a violent shiver.

"Who are . . ." I couldn't even finish. My mind rebelled at the sight before me.

Standing in the doorway was . . . *Arthur*. He held Excalibur in one hand and the other clutched a bundle of fabric to his abdomen.

The Arthur in the room hissed and recoiled, backing into the center of the room.

Galahad wasted no time and plunged his sword into our king's back.

A scream ripped from my throat and my hands flew over my mouth. My knees went weak and I staggered against the bed. *Arthur. My Arthur.* Goddess, no. I couldn't tear my eyes from the blood seeping from his back, from his strong muscled form now crumpled on the ornate carpet. In some corner of my mind, I registered that something foul was afoot, that there was another Arthur I needed to concern myself with—whether he the true or false Arthur. But I was riveted with terror at the sight of my king, my love, dead before me.

And then he changed. A garbled gasp escaped me as Arthur's body shimmered and twisted, transforming into something else. A naked woman, her hair short and dark.

I shook my head as horror paralyzed me. My body grew numb and my sluggish mind fought a raging current of grief and confusion and terror. It was like my horrible dream within a dream—blurring my sense of reality.

"What the fuck is going on here?" I croaked, ripping a sheet from the bed and covering myself up.

But no one answered. We were wrapped in our own worlds: Arthur sagged against the door jamb, his face twisted in pain, while Galahad stared at the sword in his hand, as if he had never seen this particular blade before.

Lancelot and Percival appeared in the doorway, naked from head to toe. Their bare skin registered dimly in my mind. Galahad was the only one present who was clothed.

Lancelot threw up an arm, his blue eyes widening.

Oh yes. The fire.

Arthur turned toward his knights. "Percival?" he asked.

"Got to him in time," Lancelot said. "Galahad?"

"Killed another. Not sure if this faerie is the last."

Lancelot coughed, stumbling forward. The flames were licking from floor to ceiling now, the heat of the blaze warming my cheeks. "Let's get the hell out of here!"

No one moved. I couldn't seem to summon my limbs. Or banish from my mind the image of Galahad's sword piercing through Arthur. But that hadn't been Arthur. *This* was Arthur. And he was injured.

"Now!" barked Lancelot, and then he clapped his hands. The loud noise startled me back to myself and I scrambled around the bed to retrieve my clothes and armor. Then I collected the spear, in case it was poisoned and a remedy was needed.

Galahad sheathed his sword and crossed to Arthur's side, throwing Arthur's arm around him.

Arthur cried out, but let Galahad help him into the hallway.

We retrieved clothes and armor and boots and saddlebags and then carried them all downstairs in messy bundles, the oily black smoke from the fire stinging our eyes and filling our nostrils.

In the hallway, we took a moment to dress. As Galahad helped Arthur into his tunic, I caught sight of Arthur's wound. Blood leaked freely from a puncture wound in his lower abdomen. Fear gripped me with iron fingers, ripping at my already ragged nerves. If the weapon had pierced an internal organ—the injury could be fatal.

"Ye need to stitch the wound," I said. "He's losing too much blood."

Sweat beaded Arthur's pale face.

"I can't do it here or he'll die in the blaze before he has time to bleed out," Galahad countered.

"The blacksmith's," I said, an idea seizing me. "The forge was just a few streets down. We passed it on the way here. A smithy will have water and fire to sterilize your needle."

Galahad nodded and tried to help Arthur back to his feet.

But Arthur's knees buckled beneath him.

Galahad swooped our king up in his huge arms as though cradling a child.

Arthur grunted in protest, but then his eyelids fluttered shut as blessed unconsciousness took him.

"Get the horses and meet me there," Galahad said.

My thoughts roiled like a tempest as we hurried across the dark courtyard toward the stable where we had left our mounts. The sky was still pitch black above us, without even a sliver of moon. Strange. A moon was present earlier. I looked back at the forbidding castle. An orange glow shone from the upper windows. The fire was spreading, though the flames would likely just eat up the contents of the castle and scorch the thick stones. We should be safe in the village.

"Does anyone know what in the hell happened back there?" Percival finally asked.

I let out a desperate laugh of relief as tears prickled at the corners of my eyes. My ragged nerves felt like wool pulled thin for spinning. One stiff tug and the threads would part forever.

"Faeries attacked us," Lancelot said, striding into the dim stable. His face was thunderous, his dark brows scrunched. "I can only assume that Morgana had something to do with this night."

"Or perhaps someone else doesn't want us to get the Grail?" Percival asked.

"Possible. In the end, I'm not sure it matters. They disguised themselves with glamour. Only the adder stone could see through the magic. That's how Galahad knew . . . that a faerie was atop me."

"Who did the faerie impersonate?" I asked. It had been Arthur for me, but who did the other knights think was lying with them?

Percival and Lancelot both quickly looked away from me, their cheeks noticeably reddening in the dark.

"Oh." A blush rose on my own face as well.

Percival kicked Kit's stall, causing his horse to toss his head. "Idiot! I almost ruined everything! I should have been stronger, should have pushed her away. But she was so . . . convincing." Percival closed his eyes briefly. "Lancelot, if ye hadn't come in . . . I was ready to break my vow."

"Hurry," Lancelot said gruffly to Percival, before pushing into his own horse's stall. "Don't blame yourself, Percival. Stronger men than you have been fooled by the sídhe." A dark look flashed across his eyes. "Even ones who know better."

We tacked our horses quickly and then Lancelot saw to Llamrei while I saddled Galahad's huge charger. The familiar motions soothed me, providing something else to focus on besides the memories flashing before me. I had fought in battles that stayed with me for a time, my mind replaying images of a memorable face—perhaps a kill, sometimes a fiann mate—as the light faded from the warrior's eyes. But this night would haunt me for all my days.

We found Galahad at the empty blacksmith's shop, an unconscious Arthur laid out on a table.

Lancelot handed Galahad his medical kit, and then we stepped back to let him work. I grabbed Percival's hand, who grabbed Lancelot's. Despite the oppressive heat Galahad had stoked from the forge, no one seemed willing to leave the presence of the others, to venture out into the darkness of the night. I didn't think I would ever let my knights out of my sight.

When Galahad was done, he covered Arthur

with a spare tunic and then plunged his hands into a bucket of water before collapsing onto a stool.

He shoved his blond locks out of his face. At some point, numerous strands had fallen from the leather tie he normally wore them in. "I told you all not to eat the food," he said quietly.

"The food wasn't enchanted," Lancelot snipped. "The lot of us were just drunk. Still, we can all agree this night falls firmly into the Galahad-told-us-so category."

"Will he . . . live?" I let go of Percival's hand and crossed the room to take in Arthur's sleeping form. I couldn't help myself and reached out to push the hair off his sweaty brow.

"I don't think the spear hit any organs," Galahad said. "He needs time to rest. But knowing Arthur, he'll want to move as soon as he's awake."

"The spear continues to weep blood," I said. I held the spear up and we watched as a drip fell from the head's tip down the rowan wood shaft. "Is it poisoned?"

"Just bloody faerie magic," Lancelot muttered. "Literally."

"Can he travel?" Percival asked, looking at Arthur once more. "I'm not eager to linger here any longer."

"If we take it slow," Galahad said. "He'll need food, and we don't have any here."

"Then," Lancelot said. "When Arthur wakes, we ride for Caer Benic."

I trailed my fingers along Arthur's temple, his jaw. I didn't want to stop touching him—assuring myself that he was real and alive. That is, alive for now. I sent up a prayer to the Mother Goddess and tried to infuse my strength with Arthur's. *Heal, My King*, I thought over and over and over again.

"At least there's one small silver lining," Galahad said.

"Aye? What's that?" Percival asked.

Galahad pulled his sword from its scabbard and held the blade up for us to see. The metal seemed to catch the light in a way that caused the sword to glow, and I squinted. Then blinked. This new sword was gorgeous. The slick sheen of the metal blade and cross-guard was covered in intricate knots and swirls, like the tattoos gracing Lancelot's shoulders and arms. And, set in the pommel was a violet stone the size of a quail's egg.

Percival's eyes went wide, and he crept toward the sword in awe. "Where did ye find this?"

Galahad shrugged. "When I killed the last faerie, the one in Fionna's room, my sword just . . . transformed."

A delighted laugh escaped from Percival. "We were due for a little good news, and this is good news indeed. For this isn't any ordinary sword, ye ken? This is the Grail Sword."

Chapter Twenty-Six

Lancelot

Lancelot stared at the smithy's ceiling from his bedroll. The third curse loomed heavy in his thoughts, a relentless weight pressing him down. He had one bloody job on this bloody quest—to not sleep with Fionna. And he had bloody gone and done it. True, by some twisted miracle of dark magic, the Fionna he had slept with hadn't been Fionna. And no, he hadn't been in his right mind, addled with enchanted food and wine instead. But none of that mattered. What mattered is that *he had thought the woman was Fionn*a. And he had bedded her *anyway*. He didn't care about Arthur or Caerleon or anything that moment, only the overpowering urge within him to claim her for his own. All his weaknesses, all his fears had come home to roost. And now he knew one thing, as sure as the sun rose and set each day.

He couldn't be trusted.

The reality of what he had to do slammed into him, robbing the breath from his lungs. Arthur was wounded, they were about to complete the final leg of their journey . . . and Lancelot needed to leave. He had turned the problem over a dozen ways in his mind, and each time the calculations spit out the same result. He needed to go far away from Fionna. For if he remained here, sooner or later he would give in to his weakness—again—and doom them all.

The other knights had fallen into an uneasy sleep, their bedrolls splayed about the blacksmith's forge. The fire had burned down, but still pleasantly warmed the space. Now was his chance. If he were truly going to do this, he needed to do it now.

Quiet as a mouse, Lancelot gathered his belongings, hoisting his saddlebags onto his shoulder. The door creaked in the unnatural silence and he cringed. He glanced over his shoulder, relaxing a notch when he saw that the other knights hadn't stirred, not even a little.

The cold air kissed his face, a chill wind tousling the locks of his hair. His steps dragged, as if his boots were mired in mud. Gods, he didn't want to do this. Arthur would think Lancelot had betrayed him. And so soon after Fionna's own betrayal . . . and while weakened from injury and from Morgana and her sisters' machinations. Lancelot cursed himself, cursed his weakness, cursed the third curse. He hung his saddlebags over the stall door and grabbed his horse's bridle. Cheval flicked his ears towards him.

"If only I were stronger," Lancelot murmured. *None of this would have happened,* Lancelot finished internally. His weakness had set all of this into motion. But no more. He refused to let his weakness drive the final nail into Caerleon's coffin. Or Arthur's.

Where would he go? Lancelot chewed on his bottom lip, indecision washing over him and churning in his gut. Caerleon—and Arthur—was the only home he had ever known. Perhaps he could come back some day, if he found a way to break the curse. An idea struck him like a bolt of lightning. His foster mother. Her home on the Isle of Man was a different form of misery, her care of him best described as detached aloofness. But she was wise and ancient and skilled in the ways of magic. Perhaps she knew a way to break this wretched curse. Then he could return to Caerleon and beg his king's forgiveness.

His relief was like a sudden sunburst. This didn't have to be exile. A quest of his own. To protect Arthur and his kingdom. Lancelot buckled his horse's girth and secured his saddlebags.

He led Cheval out of the stall, closing the gate behind him.

"Where do ye think ye're skulking off to?" A quiet female voice asked from the stable door.

Lancelot whirled to find Fionna, arms crossed and eyes narrowed.

"I need to take care of something," Lancelot said gruffly, trying to walk past her.

She took a step to the side and blocked his path. "Yer king lies injured, we're a day from the Grail, and *you need to take care of something*?" Her voice grew shrill. "What, ye forgot ye left the washing hanging out in the yard?"

"It's personal," Lancelot said, glaring at her. Didn't she understand this was hard enough without her trying to convince him to stay? Even as she stood before him, furious and fierce, he felt his resolve growing soft while his cock grew hard. He clenched his jaw and toed the stable floor with his boot. This was exactly why he needed to leave—he couldn't be trusted around her.

"Arthur will try to find ye." Fionna grasped his elbow with an iron grip. Gods, she was beautiful when she was angry. "It'll derail the quest. Caerleon will suffer days more. Is this what ye want?"

"Of course not," Lancelot said. "That's why I need to go."

"What of Percival?" She asked, arching an eyebrow.

"What of him?" He snapped back.

"Do not pretend yer feelings for him are false too."

Lancelot looked out into the night, his heart pounding hard against his ribs. "They're not."

"Please . . ." Her voice softened. "I don't want ye to go."

Lancelot's fingers fisted around the reins to keep them from straying to her face, her hair, to pull her lush form hard against his. His voice was hoarse when he responded. "And that is even more of a reason to go."

She stiffened, hurt flaring in her eyes.

He held his tongue against the apology struggling to break free. It was better if he hurt her than be with her. For then he would hurt them all.

"I thought . . ." she cleared her throat, looking at her boots. "I thought ye desired my love. That we had moved past whatever distaste ye had for me. But now . . . have I done something to offend ye? To earn yer ire?"

Her words twisted his heart. Didn't she see how she was perfect for him—for them? That everything she did, who she was . . . It was as if she were custom-crafted to become the final piece of their puzzle. Fitting perfectly between them, linking them all together in bonds stronger than oaths or duty.

Bonds of love.

"You did nothing wrong," Lancelot whispered. "The fault is mine, a burden I must bear."

"Then tell me. Let me share this burden." She reached up and cupped his face. And he felt his head tilting in an unconscious motion, longing to melt against the comfort of her fingers. They were as soft as velvet yet calloused from years of fighting—just a small glimpse of the dichotomy that was their Fionna.

The need to share the truth of Morgana's curse roared within him. The secret was an animal that desperately wanted to be free of its barbed cage. He ached for Fionna to understand why he pushed her away, to see that he never meant to hurt her—not then, not now.

Fionna seemed to sense his weakening and soldiered on. "At least, tell me where ye go and why. Let me explain yer decision to our king, to keep him from doubting yer loyalty. Whatever is troubling ye so, ye need not carry this weight alone any longer."

Lancelot's throat tightened. Carrying this secret made him weary to his bones. He didn't want to carry this burden this alone anymore either.

"There's another curse." The words exploded out of him, tumbling from his mouth as if they had been waiting to do so all his life.

Fionna drew herself up, her silver brows scrunching together.

"When Morgana learned of my infidelity, her sisters cursed Excalibur and Caerleon, but Morgana cursed me."

"What curse?"

Lancelot recited Morgana's cruel words, the words branded on his heart. "Never again will you know the pureness of love that flows between one man and one woman. There will be a woman, a Gwenevere pure like the white of driven snow." He paused a beat, softening his voice as tears began to gather. "You will long for her with all your heart. Perhaps she will love you too. But, if you join as man and woman, she will not only bring your downfall, but the downfall of all you love."

Fionna's mouth set in a grim line. "I don't understand."

"Don't you see?" Lancelot struggled to slow his ragged breathing, to keep the tears from falling. "*You are the Gwenevere pure like the white of driven snow. I long for you with all my heart. But if I join with you as one man and one woman, it will bring the downfall of all I love.*"

Fionna shook her head. "A Gwenevere is a sorceress. A fae enchantress. I am not a Gwenevere. I'm the daughter of Brin and Catríona Allán. Princess of Clann Allán." She tilted her head and then whispered, "Ye are mistaken, Lance."

"It's you, Fi. It has to be you. There is power dormant within you that even I don't understand. Your connection to us, the Grail, the sídhe . . . you're the foretold Gwenevere."

"Then we will not lie together," Fionna said, nodding to herself. "A simple solution."

Lancelot ran a trembling hand through his hair, his eyes darting about wildly. "I've thought of every option, every possibility, I've even tried it all! Why did you think I pushed you away, and then kept you at arm's length? But I'm weak." He drew in a quivering breath and choked out, "I long for you with all my heart. So much so, I laid with you!"

Fionna's brows pushed together. "I would remember such a beautiful moment with ye."

"I didn't join with *you*, but a dark faerie glamoured as you in that . . . that castle of maidens!" He thrust out his arm and pointed to the smoldering castle up on the hill. "But I didn't know that then! And I didn't care. As far as I knew, last night, by making love to someone I thought was you, I was bringing the downfall of myself, Arthur, Caerleon, all of us. I was triggering the third curse."

"Did you say *a third curse*?" A new voice rasped from the darkness outside the stable door. A voice he recognized. Their king's voice.

Chapter Twenty-Seven

Arthur

third curse. Morgana had mentioned this, but Arthur had ignored her taunting babble. He didn't want to believe his half-sister, for he had curses enough to contend with.

His side throbbed as though the Norse fires of Hel pulsed within him, every movement blistering agony. But when his eyes had fluttered open to see Fionna slipping out the door, he had to follow. After what happened with Excalibur . . . a cynical part of him feared she was still not trustworthy. And then he discovered that it was Lancelot—his brother, his second-in-command—who was leaving.

"My King, you shouldn't be up without assistance." Fionna hurried to his side and wedged her shoulder under his arm to support his weight. But he ignored her. He didn't need to sit down. He needed answers.

"How could you not tell me?" Arthur asked

Lancelot. "If there was a danger to my kingdom, I had the right to know. I am king!" The sudden surge of blood to his face left him lightheaded and woozy. Fionna's small frame staggered under his weight, and she steadied herself.

"Arthur—" she murmured, but it was Lancelot who filled Arthur's vision.

Guilt twisted Lancelot's face. "In a hundred years, I still could not atone for how sorry I am, Arthur. You took me in, you were a brother to me—the only family I have, really—and I repaid your kinship with ruin and destruction to your land. The other curses weighed so heavily upon your shoulders. I simply didn't want to burden you with something more to worry about."

"Bullshit," Arthur snapped. "You didn't want to admit that you failed again."

"I'm trying to make this right," Lancelot shot back. "It's why I'm leaving. I'm separating myself from Fionna, so I'm no longer a danger. I plan to visit Vivien and see if there's a way to break this curse upon me."

"*You* are *my* knight, and *you* are sworn to obey *me*," Arthur grit between clenched teeth. "And *you* do not leave without *my* permission"—he pointed a finger at Lancelot's chest—"The standing stone said the *blessed five* would find the Grail, which Merlin confirmed. Remember? That's why we forgave Fionna, even when she betrayed us."

Lancelot's face paled and he felt Fionna suck in a sharp breath at his cutting words. But Arthur's anger was too powerful a tide to be concerned for how his words affected others just now. The fury writhed within him, the betrayal a monster waking to life, sweeping him away.

"But you didn't think of that, did you?" He hurled at Lancelot's feet. "Your vision is consistently so narrow, so myopic, that you rarely consider how your actions will cost others." Arthur grimaced at a stab of pain while Lancelot's gaze hardened, as if each word fell upon him like whipped lashes. Drawing in a slow, steadying breath, Arthur continued. "You're supposed to be a leader of men, but leadership takes sacrifice. And to sacrifice, you must care for something other than yourself!"

"I love you, Arthur," Lancelot softly spoke. "And Caerleon, and our sword-brothers, and Fionna. And *that* is why I was leaving tonight."

"You can't leave until we complete the quest. I forbid it. After we drink from the Grail, your life is yours to ruin as you please. But not a minute before!"

Lancelot's hands curled into fists at his side, his jaw working. "As you command, Your Majesty."

"Now will you sit down?" Fionna asked in an exasperated voice.

"Fine," Arthur answered stiffly, and Fionna helped him to a bench in the corner of the stable, where he sat with a groan. "Wake Galahad . . . and Percival . . . We ride for . . . Caer Benic," Arthur managed through pain-laced breaths.

"Now?" Fionna asked. "Is that such a—"

"Now!" Arthur barked. It was time to finish this.

As they passed through the old city wall of Eiden's Burgh, the land around them transformed. Gone were the fog and darkness that had shrouded the city, and instead, countryside as bright and fair as Caerleon unfolded before them. Before Caerleon's curse, that was. They rode through green fields as flocks of sparrows swooped overhead. A rabbit with a bushy white tail darted in front of them in a zig-zag pattern.

Arthur held himself woodenly against the rocking movement of Llamrei's gait. A trickle of blood seeped from his wound and pooled on his breeches. But he said nothing. He couldn't stop now. Not when they were so close. He feared that if he stopped, he would never arrive at Caer Benic.

They had mapped out a distance and direction from Castellum Puellarum based on the enchanted signpost near Betws-y-Coed. But in the end, they hadn't needed the coordinates. For the beautiful blade—the one that had magically replaced Galahad's—possessed a mind of its own. Galahad held the Grail Sword loosely in his hand as they rode, and if they roamed off course, the sword tugged at him insistently, directing them onto the correct path.

"Don't know where the in hell this blade came from," Galahad said, "but I'm glad it's here."

Arthur let out a wheeze of a laugh, which sent pain shooting through his abdomen. The pain was so powerful, it took his breath away. He prayed they were almost there.

They rode up into craggy, boulder-strewn foothills of Alba. The shining expanse of the sea stretched far in the distance.

Lancelot hadn't uttered a single word since their exchange in the stable. Arthur knew his words were harsh to his friend, even cruel. But anger still burned within him. Lancelot should have trusted Arthur to handle the truth of this third curse. How weak must Lancelot think him?

A shiver wracked Arthur and he gripped his saddle, struggling to stay upright on Llamrei's back. He had been tricked by the faerie maidens in the castle too. But of all in their party, only he had been injured. So, maybe he really was the weak one.

The horses were puffing when they reached a plateau atop a hill. Galahad's sword pointed straight down as though drawn to a lodestone. He reined his horse in and peered over his shoulder.

"Is the Grail Sword broken?" Fionna asked. "Confused?"

Percival shook his head. "Nae, lass. I feel the pull here too. I think . . . we're here."

"There is no 'here,'" Arthur said. "The sword can't be right."

Galahad turned his horse in a circle, pointing the blade's tip in every direction. The sword rebelled against him, continuing to point down. As if they were supposed to come this far and no farther. "Any brilliant ideas?" Galahad asked.

Fionna furrowed her brow. "Haven't we learned that things aren't always as they seem? Especially when it comes to this quest? Percival, do you have the adder stone?"

Percival pulled the talisman out of his tunic and moved to hand the gem over. But as he did, he stilled.

"Fionna is right," he said. "Look."

Fionna took the stone from him and her eyes grew owlish. "My goddess!"

She handed the relic next to Arthur. His jaw dropped. For before him was something more extraordinary than he had ever seen in his life. A castle that floated upon the air. Huge and tall, with soaring white stone spires. No mortal had formed this keep. Relief rushed through him. They had made it—finally.

Galahad dismounted and crossed over the grass to Arthur and took the stone. He blew out a whistle and then tossed the stone to Lancelot. The giant of a knight moved to help Arthur off his horse and Arthur toppled sideways, the earth spinning beneath him.

"Bloody hell," Galahad said as he caught Arthur and helped him to the ground. "Your stitches have failed? Have you been bleeding all this time? You should have told us! We would have stopped."

"We finish this," Arthur rasped.

Galahad grumbled.

Fionna dismounted and knelt at Arthur's side, her hands fluttering over the wound. "Arthur," she said, his name soft and tender on her lips. "Ye need to take care of yerself."

"I have to take care of Caerleon," Arthur said. "If we get the Grail, the sacred vessel will heal me. So, let's get the fucking Grail."

Percival nodded. "The Blessed Grail is rumored to have healing powers."

"There's only one problem. How do we get up there?" Fionna asked.

Galahad pulled Arthur up in his arms and they walked forward.

Fionna took the stone once more from Lancelot. "There's a doorway. Here on the ground. But . . . I don't understand. It's a door to . . . nothing." She passed the talisman to Arthur and he squinted to focus.

She was right. A single door stood on the Scoti moor, with nothing behind the entryway but air and heather. The door made little sense. But they had passed beyond the realm of the logical, and into the fantastical. "We go through the door," Arthur said. "It's not the strangest thing we've seen on this quest."

The knights walked forward in a tight clump. When they reached the door, they paused. No one seemed to want to be the first to open the entry to the Grail Castle.

"You go first, Fisher heir," Galahad gestured with his head toward the large, carved oaken door.

"Great," Percival said. "I always wanted to be blasted by dragon fire or some other trap first in our party." But he wrapped his fingers around the doorknob and turned. Then he jiggled the handle and pushed. But the door didn't budge. "Locked," Percival said with a shrug.

Lancelot groaned and spun in an angry circle, but thankfully said nothing. Especially weakened how he was, Arthur had little patience for Lancelot's pessimism.

Percival was throwing his shoulder against the

door now, but the entry held firm.

Arthur looked at the space where the door was, wishing his mind was more lucid, wishing he could burn through this fevered haze that was swallowing him whole. A locked door. They needed a key. Arthur let out an incredulous laugh that quickly turned into a cough.

"Easy," Galahad said.

"Could it be that simple?" Arthur said. "Put me down."

"But Your Majesty—" Galahad protested.

"Put. Me. Down," Arthur commanded. For whatever the Grail Quest had taken from him, he wouldn't let it take his dignity. He would walk through that door on his own two feet and face whatever he found there.

Arthur reached into his belt pouch and withdrew the bone key.

"Ye think . . ." Fionna trailed off.

"All I know is here lies a locked door and we have a key."

Leaning heavily on Galahad, Arthur limped to the door. Percival handed him the adder stone and the smooth wood finish of the door materialized before him, carved with faerie runes.

With a shaking hand, Arthur slid the ivory key into the lock. The knob turned with a click, and then the door swung open.

Chapter Twenty-Eight

Percival

The Grail Castle was empty, but not the haunted emptiness of the castle they had fled in Eiden's Burgh. This emptiness felt hushed and right. A quiet anticipation. As if the place was waiting for the rightful master's return. Percival's stomach clenched and unclenched. He wiped his clammy palms on his tunic. Part of him couldn't believe that they were actually here. That he now walked the quiet halls his father had once walked. That Percival had also once gamboled through, a cheerful and tumbling boy with a shock of red hair.

Memories flashed within him as they passed through the long corridor to the Great Hall, where his father had entertained nobles and dignitaries, human and fae alike.

His feet moved of their own volition, towing him forward.

"You know the way?" Galahad asked. The Grail Sword was in his hand—that same strange glittering thing with the violet pommel. Percival knew the sword was important. He knew the Grail Sword was tied to this place, the Blessed Grail, the whole sordid legacy. The same way he was.

"Aye," Percival said. "We should find the vessel up here."

Arthur was leaning heavily on Galahad, his pallor ashen and his face beaded with sweat.

Percival prayed what they found within the Great Hall was friendly, for Arthur couldn't take another setback. He feared his king wouldn't last much longer.

Down the long hallway stretched an arching set of double doors. "There," Percival said. "The Grail should be behind those doors."

The knights' footsteps sounded ominous on the polished stone floors.

Percival's breath was tight in his chest as he reached the entry, and paused. "Are we ready?" He asked with a crooked grin.

"On with it," Lancelot barked. "We need to get Arthur healed."

Percival pushed the door open, his mouth parting. At the sight before them, they let out a collective groan.

"Another feast?" Fionna asked, her hand flying to her stomach.

A glittering array of food and drink, much like they had just left the day before, adorned a large banqueting table. But for one notable difference. A woman. Tall, lithe and fair, the woman's golden-blonde hair fell in soft waves down to her narrow waist. She wore a dress of a deep violet hue, her waist cinched with a belted girdle of golden links encrusted with amethysts. And her brow was crowned with a gold diadem boasting an amethyst stone that perfectly matched the gem on the pommel of Galahad's sword.

This, Percival was certain, was the Grail Maiden.

Percival scrambled into a bow and the others followed suit, Arthur with an audible groan.

"Fair knights. Kind king," she said. Her voice was soft and melodious, like the bubble of a fountain. "Welcome to Caer Benic. I have been waiting for you."

"We have been waiting to get here," Percival said. "Thank ye fer yer service in guarding the Blessed Grail."

"The honor is mine. I know these are dark times, and I felt it right to do what little I could to assist your righteous cause."

"The standing stone?" Percival asked. "Ye left that for us, didn't ye?"

She inclined her head in an affirmative.

"And the sign-post?" Fionna asked.

She nodded again. "This castle has been too long without her rightful king. Welcome home Percival of Caer Benic, Fisher King."

"It's good to be home," Percival said, his voice catching in his throat. However bloody and unpleasant his past had been, at least he had lived up to his father's legacy in this small way. He had done it. He had found the castle. And the Grail.

"Keeper of the Grail," Fionna began. "Our king is grievously wounded. I do not mean to be forward, but may we see the Grail and heal him? I fear he grows weaker with each passing candle mark."

The Maiden turned to survey Fionna with an appraising eye. Did her violet eyes widen as she took Fionna in? "I did not expect a Gwenevere, though perhaps I should have," the Maiden said.

Fionna winced at the title, but soldiered on. "He was pierced through with this spear, which has continued to weep blood ever since. Is the tip poisoned?"

"No. This is the sacred spear of Lleu, which weeps blood. A blessed relic of the fae to harm sovereign-blessed kings." She took the spear from Fionna's hands and the magical weapon disappeared. "We thank you for the spear's safe return. And, I am afraid the Grail does not heal mortal flesh, but I do have something that will help. Go to the table and fetch one of the red apples. They hail from the Isle of Man, from Manannán mac Lir's orchard, and possess healing properties. One bite should be enough to save the Little Dragon King."

"The sea god who delivers souls to the afterlife?" Fionna asked, mouth parted in horror.

"Yes, Princess." The Grail Maiden tilted her head prettily. "He may care for the dead, but he does not usher in death like The Morrígan. I assure you, his tree of life shall heal your king. The Lady of the Lake ferried his apples to me, should you have need of them."

Fionna studied the Grail Maiden a few wary heartbeats and then did as instructed, hurrying down the long table, her eyes searching for an apple amongst the arrayed bounty. She found one and grabbed the fruit, jogging back to Arthur.

His head was nodding now as consciousness slipped from him. "Arthur," she said, her hand stroking his sweaty brow. "Wake up, my love." She patted his face.

He jerked to alertness, but his eyes were unfocused. "Fionnabhair?"

"Eat Arthur, the apple will heal you."

She held the apple up to his mouth and he took a tiny bite.

"Chew," she encouraged, as if to a young child. "Swallow yer bite completely."

He did as instructed—a cooperative patient.

The effect was instantaneous. Arthur's color flushed and turned to the rosy pink of health. His back straightened and he let out a shuddering breath, shaking his head as if to clear the fog. He took another bite, chewing. His green eyes flew open, clear and verdant as the rolling grassy hills on a summer's day.

Gratitude and relief washed over Percival.

"Thank ye so much," Fionna said, tears glimmering in her eyes.

The Maiden nodded. "The least I can do for the sovereign-blessed king. Today is not his time. He has much left to do. Now, let us discuss your quest at Caer Benic." She looked meaningfully at Percival.

"Och!" Percival said. "The Grail." That's right. There were words he needed to speak. The very ones drilled into him as a young child. In his excitement of being here, he had completely forgotten. He cleared his throat. "What is the Grail and whom does it serve?"

The Maiden nodded approvingly. "The Blessed Grail is a sacred bowl, a vessel to grant life, and the Grail serves Arthur Pendragon of Caerleon, the rightful King over all of Briton." She waved her hand across the table, and a pile of fruit disappeared, revealing a silver bowl with engraved mythical creatures who danced around an orchard. She lifted the dish with both hands, and then offered the vessel to Percival. "I gift you the Blessed Grail."

Arthur's eyes were gleaming. "We must drink. To heal the wicked curse that has befallen Caerleon by Morgana and her sisters."

The Maiden peered kindly at Arthur. "To heal the land, you must drink from the land's life source, the land's blood. Drinking from the Grail would not be enough. There is a Chalice Well at the foot of Glastonbury Tor. If you dip the Grail into the holy waters of Avalon, and drink from her Red Spring, the Blessed Grail will do what you seek."

"Glastonbury Tor?" Arthur said with dismay. For the Tor was days' travel from here.

A shadow fell over her face. "But I cannot allow the Blessed Grail to leave Caer Benic. For the sacred vessel may fall into the wrong hands and I would be unprotected. Especially now that the Fisher King has returned and the way to the castle is unlocked."

The knights exchanged troubled glances.

"Perhaps you could come with us?" Lancelot asked.

"No, my charge is over the castle and the Grail."

"Perhaps I could offer you this," Galahad said, stepping forward. He held the sword out to her.

"Would this be sufficient to protect you?"

"The Grail Sword." Her eyes glittered with a dancing light. "How did you come upon my blade, kind Sir?"

He shrugged. "The sword kind of just appeared."

She took the blade from him reverently, stroking the handle's leather. "Yes, I think this would be sufficient enough. I can lend you the Grail for a time. Though the vessel belongs here, in Caer Benic. As does the Fisher King," she said, looking meaningfully at Percival.

"Och, lass. Well, I still have duties to attend to with His Majesty," Percival said. "But I'll return. Never fear, fair Maiden."

A smile flashed across her face. "As long as you know your place is here, Your Highness."

"Of course."

"We must depart post haste," Arthur said. "Glastonbury Tor is in Wessex. A week's journey to be sure, and a dangerous one at that since we'll have no choice but to travel through Anglo-Saxon lands. Who knows how bad the curse in Caerleon will be by then."

"Perhaps I can help," the Grail Maiden said. "The paths across the Otherworld are often shorter than their mortal counterparts. I see you are familiar with walking the immortal realms already."

The knights looked at each other in mutual confusion. "What do you mean?" Arthur asked.

"The mist clings to you. You have just arrived from the Otherworld, have you not?" She stepped toward Arthur, a soft smile on her lips. "The ivory you carry? The Bone Key allows you to move in and out of the Otherworld at will, including the *In-Between*."

Percival wanted to smack himself for not thinking of this sooner. "Castellum Puellarum, Eiden's Burgh. This village wasn't empty—drained of people. Nae, we weren't in the real village. We were in its Otherworld shadow."

Arthur huffed an irritated sigh. "That explains quite a lot, actually." To the Grail Maiden, he said, "We are not eager to enter that shadow realm again. However, if the Otherworld shortens our journey, then show us the way, Maiden."

She nodded. "I believe I can open a door directly to Avalon. You will hardly need to step foot in the Otherworld."

"Avalon?" Arthur asked.

"Yes, Little Dragon King. Glastonbury Tor is the gateway to Avalon, where the Mother Goddess herself dwells."

"Our gratitude to you, Maiden," Arthur said with a sweeping bow.

The Grail Maiden crossed to the other side of the room, to a bare stretch of stone wall. She passed her hand across the stones and the wall shimmered into a door.

Percival's mouth fell open. He wasn't sure he would ever grow familiar with magical sightings every day. As if the unnatural were as common as stewed figs.

Arthur stepped up first, opening the door before them. Through the opening lay a dim field of dead, brown grass. Oh gods. Was that Wessex?

"Once more, I thank you for your aid," Arthur said. "Caerleon is in your debt."

"You are welcome, Arthur Pendragon. I had wondered if you were indeed the king that Briton needs. But now I know that Excalibur is in capable hands."

He dipped his head into a bow and then stepped through.

Galahad was next. She patted the scabbard, which she buckled around her waist. "Thank you, fair knight. You surely must be brave and selfless, if the sword appeared to you."

Galahad stepped through.

Fionna was next. "Whatever did ye mean? Ye called me a Gwenevere. But I possess no magic. And a Gwenevere is but a faerie tale."

The Grail Maiden laid a gentle hand on Fionna's shoulder. "You have an additional quest to complete, Fionnabhair Allán. You must discover who you are. For I fear without you in all your strength, the Little Dragon King will not be able to do what must be done."

"How do I even begin such a quest?"

"Look into your past. Across the Irish Sea. It is time to look to your home, Princess."

Fionna drew in a quiet breath and then stepped through.

Lancelot was next. A dark look shadowed each handsome feature, an expression Percival knew well. His friend was angry, through Percival wasn't sure why. Perhaps he was angry over this third curse.

"Lancelot du Lac," the Maiden said. "It is time you forgive yourself."

Lancelot's jaw worked back-and-forth and, for a moment, Percival thought he might snap at her. But he curtly nodded and then stepped through.

"Sir Percival," she said. She looked at him and reached up to caress his face with a tender touch. "You remind me so much of your father. But you have the best of your mother as well."

A hollow laugh escaped him.

"I know life has been hard on you, and much of the blame lies with her. But there was indeed good in her, before the loss of your father drove her mad."

Percival couldn't stop himself from springing at the golden-haired faerie and pulling her into an embrace. "Thank ye, Grail Maiden, for standing vigil all these years."

"It is my great pleasure. But I shall relish the return of company around here, Your Majesty."

He let out another laugh. "I will return, lass. Promise. But first there are things that I must do."

Chapter Twenty-Nine

Fionna

I stumbled out of the Otherworld's doorway, my stomach heaving. I thought I might vomit. It felt as if my soul had been wrenched from within me.

I looked back as Lancelot staggered out through the doorway after me, his hands falling to his knees as he let out a hacking cough. Behind him, Percival grew visible within the doorframe, the image like a moving tapestry. He embraced the Grail Maiden before stepping through to join us.

"Och, that was fun," Percival said through gritted teeth, stumbling sideways.

The door winked shut behind us and we surveyed the surrounding land—a sorry sight. The grass had withered and died, the trees grasping skeletons, dry and shriveled leaves piled around their trunks as though fallen Samhain wraiths. Even the sky overhead hung pallid and brown, as if the smoke from a bonfire enveloped us.

"The curse has progressed so quickly," Arthur

choked out, turning slowly in a circle, his keen eyes absorbing every nightmarish detail.

It grieved me deeply to see what had become of this beautiful territory. If this is how the Anglo-Saxon lands of Wessex now suffered, I shuddered to think of Caerleon and Briton. I thought fondly of the fertile, green rolling hills and lush, moss-draped forests that had first greeted me when I stepped off the boat from Ulster.

"How could Morgana do this?" I whispered to myself. "I thought the fae were creatures of earth."

Arthur heard me. "What my father did to my half-sisters . . . perverting any goodness they once held. I fear they are only creatures of wrath now. Creatures who desire to bring the downfall of man and whatever land supports him."

"I am beyond grieved," I said, finding his eyes. We held each other's gaze, the sadness in his tearing through my heart.

"Let us show them then," Percival said, pulling me from Arthur's intensity, "show them that mortals are no easy adversaries and not easily bested."

We stood at the foot of a massive terraced hill seeming to rise out of a desiccated marshland. Before the hill, a stone circle peeked out at us, the afternoon sun hitting a central stone in bronzed spears of dingy light. We made our way toward the large menhirs— the ancient stones—unsure of exactly where to locate the waters of Avalon. As we neared the first slope, the sound of a bubbling spring reached our ears.

Healthy, green yew trees swayed in a gentle breeze. The wind's fingers cooled my warmed skin and refreshed my spirit. For beyond the lacy boughs, a verdant garden sprawled around the reddest water I had ever seen. So red, in fact, it was as though the land were bleeding out. In a few steps, my feet stepped from golden brown death into a living wildness that rippled through my body in calming waves.

Arthur halted before what appeared to be a well and wrinkled his brow in distaste. The springs beyond were not just red, but thick. Like blood.

A chill wended down my spine as I remembered the Grail Maiden's words. *To heal the land, you must drink from the land's life source, the land's blood.*

"These are the waters of Avalon?" Lancelot said in dismay, a grimace on his face. He stood to the side, as if he were still in the Otherworld, as if he had never passed through. He was a specter, a mere shadow, his feelings transparent yet distant from us simultaneously. Since the stable in Eiden's Burgh, he had barely uttered a word. Since Arthur had dressed him down and commanded him as a soldier rather than as a friend.

The third curse offered two versions of death. Presently, he and Arthur's withering bonds of brotherhood suffered the same fate as these dying lands. I ached to show Lancelot how he was still welcome here. To show him that he was forgiven, no matter the mistakes or wrongs made. We were five. We were one. Hadn't these beautiful men shown this very care to me when I had stolen Excalibur? Now it was our turn to rise above betrayal for Lancelot. But first, we needed to absolve another curse.

Percival was surveying the spring, his brow furrowed. "Hand me the Grail, Yer Majesty?" He said to Arthur, who handed over the ornate bowl. Percival knelt before a stone lion that was carved into an ancient stone, the creature's mouth wide open. Thick, dark-red water trickled between the beast's fangs to a small pool below, as though blood dripped from its maw after a kill.

A delighted laugh escaped from him that was all Percival—joy. His heritage may be tied to the Fisher King line, but the true magic coursing through his veins was a happiness akin to the bluest of skies, sun-drenched meadows, and wildflowers dancing merrily in a melodic breeze. He stood, rays of sunshine on his lips as he brought the Grail back to us reverently. "Look!"

The water within was crystal clear, as though cupped from a mountain spring. And before any of us could stop him, he downed every last drop. And, as he did so, the land below us, down the hill, shimmered and changed. A sweet-scented wind played with Percival's copper strands affectionately before ripping through the skeletal trees, arousing the white and pink buds of spring to adorn each naked branch. The marsh grass—brown and dead—dotted with blades of green as new patches speared out from the cracked, earthen crust.

Arthur whooped like a boy and grabbed the Grail from Percival. He hurried to the spring and knelt, scooping rusted water into the vessel. Eagerly he downed the contents, clear water dribbling over his chin and onto his tunic.

The land glimmered with change once more.

New leaves unfurled along the blossomed branches—bright yellowed-greens—and the blackened bark warmed to umber hues. The glinting green of Arthur's eyes deepened as he stared about in wonder. A flock of birds alighted from nearby trees—birds, I was certain, that were not roosting there before. Patches of green grass sprang forth, as if emerging from winter's slumber to the dizzying heights of spring within a few erratic beats of my heart. In the garden around the spring, the ground gently quaked and split. Arthur anchored his feet, though the rest of us cautiously stepped back. Then, to my thundering pulse's surprise, a mighty oak grew from the small fissure in the enchanted garden. Knotted branches sprawled out in protection over the well, long limbs leafing out in seemingly endless shades of green. Arthur peered over his shoulder with a boyish grin, though his back remained straight as a king, his legs firmly planted as a warrior.

Galahad drank from the spring next and, again, the land transformed. Spring dawned much lighter now. Wildflowers in a rainbow of colors bloomed around the stone circle and carpeted the paths snaking around the marsh. Golden light pierced through the dingy sky and spilled honeyed rays across the land. And, I swore, the sun painted the very landscape from the palette of gold brushing Galahad's mane of wavy hair and skin. Even the deep blues saturating the sky reflected in Galahad's eyes.

Galahad handed the sacred dish to Lancelot, who hesitated.

"Go on," Arthur encouraged.

"You're one of us," I said softly.

Lancelot shot me a dark look, but he obeyed.

As he drank from the Blessed Grail, the land came alive as fireflies burst from the reeds as though cooling their wings in the gentle caress of an evening breeze. The flickering green and purple lights frolicked from stone to stone, sponging velvety moss in cracks and crevices. Yellow and sea-green lichen flowered on trunks, limbs, and dotted rocks. Ferns curled out from the ground and shadowed the newly sprouted grass as though a mother hen protecting her chicks. When the land rested once more, he lifted his granite-carved eyes to mine, his posture as rigid as the menhirs guarding his back.

"Fionna, you're next." Lancelot handed me the bowl. Our fingers touched, and a muscle along his jaw jumped.

"Thank ye," I whispered in reply, but he ignored me.

Drawing in a shaky breath, I knelt beside the spring, dipping the Grail into the red-tinged water. I drank deeply, the surprisingly sweet water sliding down my throat. When I lowered the bowl, I looked below us, ready to see the last patches of grass and brittle trees healed, the land surrounding the Tor as green and bright as ever.

But nothing happened. Not even the wind stirred. The land appeared the same as before I drank.

"Did I do something wrong?" I asked, looking from the spring to the bowl. "Should I try again?"

"Yes, try again," Arthur said.

So, I did, and though the water was pure on my

tongue, the land was unaffected.

Arthur spun in a slow circle, running his hands through his hair. "I don't understand. The blessed five . . . should have healed the land. Right Percival?"

"Aye, that's what the standing stone declared and Merlin confirmed." Percival frowned, a strange look on the lad's face.

"As much as it pains me to say this," Arthur began, slowly, meeting each of our expectant gazes. "Let us return to Caerleon when dawn breaks. We have accomplished much. The land has begun to heal, and we now have the Grail. Perhaps Merlin can explain what went wrong and how to completely break the curse."

The thought of returning to Caerleon warmed me. I prayed news of my father and sister awaited me there.

The other knights nodded to Arthur's suggestion and I handed the bowl back to Arthur, no longer feeling as if I deserved to touch such a sacred relic.

Unease bubbled up within me, as dark as the bloody water of the spring. Why had I failed them? If I were truly one of the blessed five, then why did the curse over Caerleon and her neighboring lands remain?

Facing Merlin's gold-ringed cambion eyes unnerved me too. *Do you have any faerie blood?* The druid's question, from the day I had visited his cave, rang loud in my mind.

More memories surfaced. Drinking the faerie wine with no ill effects. The Bone Carver grasping a lock of my hair and asking me about my power.

The Grail Maiden, just moments before, voicing a strange comment about unwittingly entertaining a Gwenevere at Caer Benic. Lancelot's certainty that I was the one tied to the prophesied third curse.

Suddenly, I was sure of nothing. Even, it seemed, who I was.

Chapter Thirty

Lancelot

ightfall's dew blanketed the magical garden around the Chalice Well and Red Spring. The droplets glistened in the fading moon light as though a dusting of black diamonds. Lancelot welcomed the remaining darkness.

Atop his bedroll, he allowed his unflappable mask to drop—the one he had held before him by sheer will alone. Now he wanted to weep. For he knew what he must do before the sun finally rose to greet the new day.

They had made camp by the gurgling spring, beneath the boughs of the giant guardian oak and beside blackthorn trees. Soon after, their horses appeared from the northern side of the garden, nickering, vapor puffing angrily from their flaring nostrils. How had they forgotten about their horses? Even more baffling, how did the horses know where to find them and arrive so soon? Faerie magic, Lancelot knew. Another debt owed to the beautiful Grail Maiden of Caer Benic. Still, the excitement of the

Grail had wiped away all reason and thought, it seemed.

Despite much coaxing, they had not been able to convince their horses to drink from the Tor's bloody waters. So, they took turns offering their mounts clear water from the ornate silver bowl, each knight cringing at the sacrilege.

Lancelot, then, laid out his bedroll far from the others. He didn't deserve to be near the fire now that his king regarded him with ice-frosted disapproval. It was fitting that Lancelot's body grew as numb as his spirit felt. Part of him wanted to rail at the unfairness of Morgana's vengeance and Arthur's judgment. He had made one mistake with Morgana. *One mistake,* and his life, all he had toiled so hard to obtain—family, recognized prestige, restoring a piece of his birthright by becoming second to the king—had been ripped from him. But he couldn't ignore the quiet voice whispering from the black corner of his mind that he hadn't made just *one* mistake. This was simply the "one mistake" exposed to the sunlight. There had been mistakes aplenty before, careless dalliances with nobles' wives and sons, or virgin maids. He had lived each day as though he were untouchable, following a path of self-indulgence and pleasure—whatever numbed his doubts over his own worthiness. But he had no more lingering doubts. This quest had shown him first-hand how unworthy he truly was.

Lancelot drank from the Grail and his act had healed the land. But that gift to his king, to the mortal lands he called home, was a thin consolation. He had never felt so useless as he did today in Caer Benic. Percival—the Fisher King—had known the phrase to summon forth the Grail's acceptance. Fionna, with her strange secrets, gave Arthur Manannán mac Lir's apple to heal his stab wound and returned Lleu's spear to the Grail Maiden. Even Galahad, a lowborn Norseman, had gained the Grail Sword through noble and valiant deeds, allowing them to take the Grail from its rightful home.

What had Lancelot offered? Nothing. *Blessed five, my arse*, he thought.

He knew that Arthur was most concerned, and rightfully so, with the remaining tendrils of poison clinging to Caerleon's waters and earth. But Lancelot's mind was consumed with the curse on him alone. Whatever good they achieved at Glastonbury Tor, he could undo it all if he gave into his weakness and lay with Fionna. And whether through trickery or magic or weakness, he couldn't guarantee their joining wouldn't happen. Not if they remained together.

Arthur had forbidden him to leave before they secured the Grail. Lancelot had honored this part of the quest. They had the Grail. He drank from the spring. Arthur Pendragon and the Knights of Caerleon didn't need him anymore.

And now there was only one solution: he must leave.

The sound of soft snores and even breathing drifted past the fire's smoldering embers to his ears—sounds he had listened to for hours while he wobbled with indecision. But now he was resolved. Lancelot's heart sank, heavy with festering grief, as he crept out of his bedroll, rolling the furs and woolen blankets up quietly. He tiptoed through the trees to where they had tied their horses and, as silently as an over-grown grave, he saddled and bridled his mount.

He knew where he should go, though he shivered at the very thought. Home. Castle Peel on the Isle of Man—the main residence of Vivien, Lady of the Lake—hadn't been much of a home compared to his time in Wales. Though distant and fickle, his foster mother was kinder than most—as far as faeries went—understanding that humans had souls and destinies and hearts. She had never once comforted him, and she sometimes forgot he even existed for days on end. But she had taught him how to fit into a world he couldn't understand. A skill that had seen him through many trials, even today's.

Vivien also possessed unnatural wisdom. She was part of the strange tangle of threads that tied Arthur to Excalibur, the Grail, and the Túatha dé Danann. Perhaps she would lend a remnant of knowledge to help Lancelot break this foul curse. Perhaps she would even take pity upon him, if he prostrated himself before her. Maybe she would favor him with help to seize back his wretched life.

Dread pooled in his stomach as the Isle of Man haunted his bruised memories. Particularly one. His first hunt with his mother's court. As a lad of ten, Lancelot had begged Vivien for weeks to attend the Great Hunt on Beltane's eve. Finally, she relented. And when a gorgeous buck came into view, his herd in tow, his foster mother's faerie retinue had crowed at Lancelot to take the shot. He plucked an arrow from his quiver, drew back the string—and missed. Instead, he hit a mother deer in the flank, wounding her grievously. The faeries, including one named Grastin, a particularly cruel sídhe male, had dragged him forward to finish his kill. Tears had brimmed in Lancelot's eyes as he regarded the spotted fawn hovering in the distance, bleating for her mother, afraid of the strange scents of man and fae. Grastin had handed a wicked hunting knife to Lancelot and demanded he kill both mother and fawn. For no baby could live without its mother.

Mocking words, Lancelot knew—even then—that were aimed at more than just the wildlife before them. The faerie courts found his mortal presence unnatural and believed Vivien should have left him for dead rather than accept his life as an offering from a weak woman who had chosen her husband's killer over her own flesh and blood.

An exiled prince he remained—not really belonging to anyone but himself.

Lancelot shook off the memory, thickly swallowing. He wasn't that boy anymore. He had only ever told one person that story. Arthur. "It was a mercy," Lancelot had said, still trying to convince himself.

"A mercy would have been the fae male killing the fawn himself," Arthur had said softly, those green eyes full of understanding. Arthur was like that. He saw a man's weakness, his vulnerability, and through a rare beauty only Arthur could possess, counted those failings as strength. And then, by his faith in those who kept his company, those perceived strengths became so. But . . . in Lancelot's case, Arthur's faith had been misplaced.

Lancelot swung into the saddle and then drank in the sight of his companions' sleeping forms beneath the giant oak, their bodies illuminated by a sliver of moonlight.

Percival, the male lover he had always wanted, yet never felt he deserved. Headstrong and impetuous and eager. His eternal, cheerful playfulness and ridiculous humor a balm to Lancelot's shadowed, insecure heart. Lancelot touched his lips in wonderment, closing his eyes and re-imagining the feel of Percival smile as he claimed Lancelot's mouth in return. The feel of stubble brushing against his lower lip. The magic dancing between Percival's breath and his. Lancelot opened his eyes and forced his gaze to move on before his decision faltered once more.

Galahad. Simple yet kind and honorable to a fault, and always ready to nurture a hurting soul through his gentle compassion. Protective and rascally like a brother too. The giant of a man was more secure in himself and his abilities than the wealthiest of nobles from the finest breeding. Around Galahad's strength, Lancelot often felt invincible. So much so, if ever Lancelot was lucky enough to know sons of his own, he wanted to name one Galahad in honor of his valiant sword-brother. Lancelot blinked back the building emotion and focused on a snowfall of swirling braids and flyaway strands strewn across a bed of furs.

Fionna. His very heart; his soul's true mate; his equal. Stronger and more beautiful than any woman he had ever known. Formidable in battle, and who loved even more fiercely—a tenacity so enduring, she would be willing to lay down her very life for those her heart claimed. Somehow, despite all his unkind acts to push her away, she still cared for him. And fought for him too. Longing for him to know the completeness of her love, even if their bodies never joined as lovers. Yearning for him to always belong—to her, to them. He thought that final truth might break him the most.

If not for Arthur. His brother.

Arthur, who had been through more betrayal and sorrow and cruelty in his twenty-two years than most men did in their lifetimes, and yet, still managed to believe the best of people and the world. Arthur was the man that men wished to be. The man Lancelot aspired to be. And the king Lancelot would always fail. His foster brother was truly the most beautiful man Lancelot had ever known and leaving him felt like death. For how could Lancelot live without his dearest friend?

And yet, he must. If he possessed any love for Arthur, he would leave and not return until he was worthy of the honor and love his brother readily bestowed upon him.

Lancelot tapped his horse's flanks and whispered, "Farewell," as he cantered forward into the gray twilight of dawn.

This time, there was no fierce Fionna or angry Arthur to stop him.

This time, there was only the last vestiges of night and the lone caw of a crow.

Interlude

Morgana

The crow watched the dark, feather-haired male's retreating form from the swirling cloud banks rolling over the green land. The rising sun gilded the terraced grass slopes as the first rays peeked over the sacred hill of Avalon. This land belonged to the Mother Goddess and formed a gateway to the Túatha dé Danann courts. Mist began to shroud the surrounding area and the crow sank farther into the streams of both natural and unnatural fog. The crow hopped onto the ground and summoned the shadows and whispers around her, transforming.

Anger burned within Morgana. Despite staying ten steps ahead of these bumbling mortals, they had almost ruined everything today. All her carefully laid plans, her time grooming that fool O'Lynn, flying back and forth across the Irish Sea. She faulted the Grail Maiden and the old gods. Those meddling creatures had all but delivered the Blessed Grail into her half-brother's unworthy hands. But despite that unexpected downturn of fortune, two delightful events had taken place. Inexplicable even to her, the Grail had failed, and her sister's curse over Caerleon remained. And even better, her curse on Lancelot had driven him from the embrace of his sword-brothers and the witch.

To her faerie ears, she could hear the faint sound of hoofbeats echoing in the air. She smiled in triumph. Lancelot thought he did what was best for his king by abandoning him. How wrong he was. Lancelot's honor was his downfall; his loyalty sealed his betrayal.

Morgana observed Arthur's camp through black unblinking lashes. She pondered the puzzle before her, turning the strange circumstances over in her mind with distaste. She had never liked puzzles or riddles. Wastes of time, childrens' games. She treasured *results*.

But she needed to solve the riddle the witch presented. Could she be wrong, and the white-haired witch wasn't the foretold Gwenevere whispered among the sídhe? A demi moon goddess of centuries past? It had seemed evident that this witch was a "gwen," a specimen so beautiful, to look upon her was a form of torture. And, yet, Lancelot had not bedded the witch, even when charmed by the necklace's enchantment. He had never resisted a beautiful man or woman before.

A dark tortured thought spasmed within her and kindled a spark of hope. Did he miss his dark fae lover? Did he miss being with a female who understood the black pain he carried deep inside his mortal heart?

Who was willing to rage and war beside him until his pain empowered them both to greatness? She shoved the thought aside ruthlessly. Lancelot did not deserve one such as her.

Morgana focused upon the woman curled up in a nest of furs by the flickering embers of last night's fire. There was something *other* that replied to Morgana's test of magic. A mortal woman did not carry such strength, prowess, or steeled beauty. Nor did she reflect moonshine in her silver gaze. Only faeborn held such elemental traits. But the Blessed Grail had failed to dissolve all curses upon her half-brother and his land. Even fae who drank from the Grail were absolved from their curses and received the Mother Goddess's blessing.

The only way the Grail could fail fae or mortal alike is if they were under the protection of a more powerful magic. But what was mightier than the Grail? Perhaps . . . a géis, a powerful spell of protection or prohibition. Could this *gwen* be protected by such an enchantment? Hidden in plain sight until a Gwenevere was needed?

If so, then the witch truly did not know of her powers and, thus, did not have access to them. It meant Morgana and her sisters still had free reign to soak in the land's death and the people's too. And it gave her time to do all she could to prevent the witch from unlocking her powers as an earth- and sovereignty-goddess.

Or . . . she could end her right now. The feathers of Morgana's dress whispered across the grass as she crept toward where the witch slept. Curls of mist clawed the ground where she knelt and unsheathed an obsidian dagger to plunge into the witch's heart, a heart as pure as the driven snow.

"Morgana?" a voice slurred from a bedroll across the cold fire. The golden-haired knight sat up and rubbed at his eyes while cracking a roar of a yawn. A sound loud enough to wake the dead, and the remaining warriors around the fire. In a single drawn breath, shadows and the greedy prayers of men tumbled around her in a dark blur.

The crow hopped away from the witch and met the golden male's confused stare. Then, she flapped her wings with a warning caw and flew into the mists of Avalon. She would allow the witch to live. For now. She would discover who sired her and the terms of the géis, before joining O'Lynn.

Satisfied with her new course, the crow cawed once more and then slipped through the mortal veil into the Otherworld.

Chapter Thirty-One

Arthur

rthur woke with the dawn, feeling stronger and more optimistic than he had in weeks. True, the curse over Caerleon wasn't completely broken, but *they had found the Blessed Grail*. A feat his father had strived to achieve for decades but never accomplished. But *Arthur* had done it. He had found the sacred vessel.

As he stretched, he felt none of the stiffness he normally did after a night of sleeping on the hard ground. The enchanted apple must have healed even the smallest of ailments. He rolled his shoulders, then covered a yawn as his eyes fell onto Fionna's stirring form.

The past few weeks felt akin to a lifetime. They had endured so much. But they had overcome every hardship. Together.

Arthur swept an appreciative gaze around the fire circle and paused. His brows furrowed. One bedroll was missing. Lancelot. Perhaps he had risen early.

Maybe practicing with his blade as he sometimes did when he couldn't sleep.

Arthur stood and wove between the trees to where they had tied the horses, his heart in his throat. Lancelot's charger was gone.

"Fool man," Arthur spat.

"Mmm?" Fionna called out. She pulled on her boots and pushed loose strands of hair out of her eyes.

Arthur spun and stalked back to their fire pit.

"What troubles ye?" she asked. When he didn't reply, she tried again. "Ye seem upset."

"Lancelot is gone."

The blood drained from her face, each delicate feature paling more than her already fair skin. "Fool man!"

Arthur loosed a dark laugh. "That's what I said."

"I considered how we needed to talk to him just yesterday. We shouldn't have let offenses remain as strong as they were in the stables."

"You think this my fault?" Arthur asked, the words sounding more defensive than he intended. In truth, Lancelot's absence probably was his fault. He had let his anger get the better of him. Though he had meant every word he said in the stable, he also understood that Lancelot's lies were a misguided attempt to protect Arthur. Lancelot may be foolish and headstrong and impulsive at times, but he was always loyal.

"I don't blame ye, My King," Fionna said. "Lancelot is a grown man. He makes his own choices. But I know this quest wore on him differently than the rest of us. He bore a dissimilar burden. And we needed to show him that, despite his failings, he was still welcome."

Percival and Galahad began to stir and were now sitting up in their bedrolls.

Galahad let out a jaw-cracking yawn, then murmured, "Do you see a pesky crow?"

"Dreaming of birds, chipmunk?" Percival asked, a puckish look on his sleepy face.

"Wait." Galahad's visage scrunched up as he looked at the sky, as if he could see into his head this way. "No, I thought I saw Morgana earlier. But then I realized it was just a crow, so I went back to sleep."

"Shit." Arthur rubbed his brow. "Lancelot is gone. We need to go after him."

"Bloody crabapple," Percival swore. A dark expression flitted across the lad's eyes before brightening to their normal earthen hue, as though a flickering lightning strike of hurt. Arthur narrowed his eyes curiously. Was his and Lancelot's kiss more than drunken games?

Fionna cut through Arthur's wandering thoughts. "Do ye have any idea where he's heading?"

"I suspect north," Arthur said with a sigh. "Toward the Isle of Man. Perhaps he seeks a way to break the curse."

"I thought ye wanted to journey to Caerleon and speak with Merlin?" Fionna countered.

"I did. But we've bought ourselves a little time." Arthur combed fingers through his short strands. "Perhaps if we are quick, we can catch him and convince him to return home with us. I'm still not certain we won't need all five of us in the end."

"Uh, I'm not sure we'll need to return to speak with Merlin," Galahad said, standing. "Isn't that him right there?"

"Or maybe another bird," Percival practically chirped. "Are ye even awake, ye big oaf?"

Arthur blinked, not sure if the sight he beheld was a mirage or some strange trick of the mystical garden. For it did appear as though his chief advisor was indeed riding up the hillside toward their camp, the morning sun shining on the bald sides of his head.

"How in the name of the goddess did he know?" Fionna gnawed the inside of her lip.

"Maybe a little bird told him," Percival said, sliding another mischievous look Galahad's way.

Galahad groaned and wacked the younger man on the backside of his head. "It's not natural to be so cheerful first thing in the morn."

"Having a druid in your court is convenient at times," Arthur said to Fionna with a hollow chuckle, ignoring the antics of his other two knights. Gods, he was glad to see Merlin. Perhaps the druid would have answers to the riddles eluding their party.

"Good morning," Merlin said, reining his panting horse to a stop. Sweat and caked mud coated his brown and white dappled stallion. The horse heaved for breath as foam gathered around the charger's mouth. How hard had he ridden his horse? And for how long? Before Arthur could ask, Merlin swung down and wrapped Arthur into an embrace.

Galahad stepped forward and led the fatigued stallion to a freshly-filled Grail.

"Good morning yourself," Arthur replied, patting Merlin's shoulder. "Not often do I have the pleasure of seeing you outside of Caerleon's grounds. To what do I owe this honor?"

"Grave tidings, My King," Merlin said. "I wish that I could allow you this moment to celebrate, for the transformation around me tells that you have indeed found the Blessed Grail."

"Yes. Though the healing is not complete. We have questions."

"All in due time," Merlin said. "First, I must give you this." He handed over a crinkled letter.

Arthur studied the missive, his eyebrows knitting together. A stone grated along the pit of his stomach. For Merlin to journey so far to deliver a message personally . . .

The other knights crowded round.

Arthur opened the letter and scanned the contents quickly. As he took in the words, his spirits sank further. "A letter from Donal O'Lynn." He looked meaningfully at Fionna. "Respectfully rejecting our offer of ransoming anything less than Excalibur. And he says for the insult of such a minuscule offer, now the price for your father has increased. Not just Excalibur. But my crown as well."

Fionna's expression pinched into rage and she spat, "That snake!" Then she faltered, a deathly calm glazing her narrowed gaze. "Wait. My father? What about Aideen?"

Arthur met her silver eyes with pity. "The letter is signed Chieftain Donal and Aideen O'Lynn."

A cold wind whipped at Arthur's cloak, tugging the heavy wool into a swirl around his body. For a moment, Arthur believed he glimpsed thunderclouds gathering in Fionna's eyes before she spun away from their group and stalked into the trees.

"Should we go after her?" Galahad asked.

"Ye first," Percival said with a shaky laugh.

Arthur watched her retreating form until she disappeared into the foliage and dusky light. "Let her be."

From the dense shield of trees, a ragged scream rent the morning chill, followed by another. Her fury seeming to billow a bitter gust of icy wind that gnashed at their exposed skin. Percival's copper hair lashed about his face like licking flames while Galahad's golden waves floated in the air.

Merlin, however, simply pulled his cloak's hood over his head, shadowing his features, save the gold-rimmed light flashing from his Otherworldly hazel eyes.

Fionna's raw grief continued, clawing at Arthur's heart, shredding what remained of his strength. His hands curled into fists, his nails digging into the flesh of his palms as her battering ram of emotions beat down his walled fortress of anger and anguish and fear.

He began to turn toward her when a sudden burst of frigid rain erupted above them from a nearly cloudless sky, splattering on Arthur's upturned forehead. Rivulets of water dripped down his cheeks and down his neck.

Quickly, he folded the letter, tucking the missive away and out of this strange, furious weather. "I should have done far more," he grit between clenched, chattering teeth. Then he released his own fury to the wind and rain, shouting, "I shouldn't have laid all my focus on the Grail! Selfish! Now, Lancelot is gone and Fionna's sister is shackled to a monster!"

Merlin pulled his cloak tighter around his gray robes. "I'm afraid, Your Majesty, there is more. The messenger returned with other tidings. O'Lynn and his new bride have been sighted with a dark-haired fae at their side. A female."

"Morgana?"

"I believe so. He spotted them last in the port of Dublin, eight days prior, where Dál nAraidi ships are massing."

Arthur grew dizzy as his heart galloped into a feral rhythm. "What are you saying?" He barely spoke above a whisper. But he already knew the answer, the stone in his gut grinding his nerves to dust.

"Your Majesty," Merlin began, holding Arthur's gaze steady. "Your stray knight will have to wait. For you must return to Caerleon and prepare for war."

To Be

Continued

Author Thanks

Thank you, Readers for giving our Arthurian Legend reverse harem tale a try. We hope you enjoyed Fionna and her brave knights! Please leave a review on Amazon, Goodreads, or wherever else online you talk books. Reviews will help other readers find our book and is a wonderful way to thank an author for entertaining you.

Writing a book takes a village! And, in this case . . . an international one :-)

As with our first book, *The Fifth Knight*, our eternal thanks to Gareth Thomson of North Lanarkshire, Scotland for helping us craft Percival's lyrical language, assisting us with historical and geographical details of Strathclyde and Edinburgh, as well as reviewing our Eiden's Burgh scenes for accuracy.

And, our hearty gratitude to fellow author Dierdre Reidy of Dublin, Ireland for reading a beta copy of *The Third Curse* to review the Irish elements in our story, including the language. Fionna is so much complex and fun because of your help!

We also appreciate Deborah Woods of Norway, Katie Kent, Erik Saulness, and Kristen Brandon of the U.S. for beta reading copies of *The Third Curse* to ensure each page was polished beautiful for you, the readers. They deserve many happy author fangirl tears of gratitude.

Also, an audiobook is also in the works for our entire series and will be narrated by Sunil Patel of London, England and a female narrator (to be announced).

All right . . . time to get back to writing :-)

Happy reading!

Claire Luana & Jesikah Sundin

Historical Notes

Hey there. This is your *Knights of Caerleon* lore keeper, Jesikah Sundin. And . . . whew! This was a doozy of a book to write, and for so many twisty-turny reasons. But for the sake of historical notes, I'm mainly going to focus on two topics: the Grail Quest and who Gwenevere was in Arthurian Legend mythos. And, because it's me, I might wander about to get there. So, hold tight.

First, if you missed the *Historical Notes* from book one, you can read all about the origins of Arthur Pendragon and Arthurian Celtic pagan lore on my blog.

Now to book two . . .

The Grail Quest. There are hundreds and hundreds of stories that make up the larger bulk of Arthurian Cycle stories. Tales that have inspired spin-off literature for centuries (just type "grail" into Amazon and you'll see what I mean). And tales that have given story fodder to Hollywood since the dawn of the silver screen. I just want you to know that it is REALLY hard to not spam this feature with Monty Python and Indiana Jones memes. Heh. I said spam. If you're not sure of why that's funny, then I suggest you look up Grail Quest inspired Broadway musicals.

And with the Grail Quest comes the equally as legendary "tests"—ones I certainly felt as I rifled through odd—mostly humorous in cringy "Go home, you're drunk Middle Ages"—story after story after story. My lore keeper's eagle eye was hunting for very specific tales, though. Ones as old as the Arthurian Legend itself. And I found three suitable candidates.

The Great Boar Hunt

A Celtic mythology staple. I encourage you to read this short Cliff's Notes version of the Twrch Trwyth story because it's hilarious (linked above). The Middle Ages are ripe with beard stories. No, seriously. But this beard story takes the hipster micro-craft beer . . . er, I mean cake. Alas, while I contemplated magical razor kits for Galahad, our gentle giant, both Claire and I kept our tale basic: faerie boar does bad things. Kill the boar!

The Bone Carver is my faerytale twist to this cornerstone Celtic mythological story. Though Bone Carvers do exist in folktales, as far as I could tell, they're not present in Arthurian lore. Boo. Well, now one certainly is *winks*.

The Afanc of Betws-y-Coed

Also known as the Addanc, this legend is another strange Celtic myth origin story that has actually shaped the history and tourist appeal of a real town nestled in the Snowdonia region of northwest Wales. Though this isn't a beard story, it is a monster beaver story. Yes. A giant, flood-inducing, people-killing beaver. *side-eyes the Middles Ages* Click on the link above for a quick pre-Arthurian *Mabinogion* read about this monstrous beaver and the lullaby-singing maiden. But, when Arthurian adventures rolled around, the original folktale was dressed up in *Peredur son of Efrawg*, a romance found within the *Mabinogion* (Peredur is Welsh for Percival). This Welsh folktale, blinged out by The Crusades, introduced a maiden who gives Peredur a "stone of invisibility" to aid in his slay-the-monster hero's feat. A monster that was no longer a giant killer beaver, but more reptilian and demonic in nature. Turns out, to Peredur's delight, that this maiden is none other than the Queen of Constantinople who is accompanied by two female mystics—sexy maidens who can raise the dead.

And, yes, in case you're curious, cannabis was really what most of the ancient world smoked until tobacco was introduced in the late Medieval period and early Renaissance. (Probably explains all the beard and monster beaver stories).

Castle of the Maidens

Ahhh, where do I even begin with this one? Perhaps the most famous of all the Grail Quest "tests" and present in every Grail cycle story. So much so, even *Monty Python and the Holy Grail* had to mock this trope with desperate young women trying to take Galahad's virginity.

Oh, I am afraid our life must seem very dull and quiet compared to yours. We are but eight score young blondes and brunettes, all between sixteen and nineteen and a half, cut off in this castle with no one to protect us! Oh, it is a lonely life -- bathing, dressing, undressing, making exciting underwear.... We are just not used to handsome knights. Nay, nay, come, come, you may lie here

(Read the rest of the Castle Anthrax scene here)

As a side note, Galahad the Chaste and Percival the Chaste are oscillating tropes as well. We chose Percival for our tale, as he seemed to have the most "holy virgin" stories of all the knights.

Soooo, originally . . . the Castle of the Maidens is the Celtic tale about The Nine Sorceresses, which is also from *Peredur son of Efrawg* in the *Mabinogion*. In this tale, these sorceresses are the armed witches of Caer Lyow. By-the-way, "The Nine Maidens" is a reoccurring trope in British/Celtic mythology. Which is how this Welsh tale ended up in Scotland. And, interestingly enough, the "Castel of the Maidens" in Scotland influenced the Welsh tale of The Nine Sorceresses. Savvy? Good. So, what was the actual Castle of the Maidens?

Edinburgh Castle. Until the 1500's, this castle was known throughout as the Maidens' Castle (Latin: *Castellum Puellarum*). Castle Rock, where the present-day castle dwells, was a site often mentioned throughout ancient texts. The problem? No one can confirm, absolutely, the historical origins of why "maidens" are truly associated with this place. Though, they do believe that young women of Picti royal heritage were kept in a structure of sorts atop

Castle Rock at some point (When? The details are murky and, thus, chronicled as "the old time"—for reals, "the old times"). But this castle is most famous for St. Margaret's Chapel, the oldest surviving building in Edinburgh. This is a stone structure built by King David I of Scotland in the 12th century for his mother, Princess Margaret, who was eventually canonized by the Catholic church.

Did they make exciting underwear there, though? Well, the verdict is still out . . . BUT, it is interesting to note that a hill near Edinburgh Castle is named Arthur's Seat.

And Glastonbury Tor? Steeped in Arthurian Legend. This location in Wessex, England is considered the origins for the Isle of Avalon. The Tor was originally surrounded by marshlands, making this sacred hill an island. Tor is an Old English word for "hill." But the Celts referred to the Tor as *Ynys Wydryn*, aka the Isle of Glass. And the famous mists of Avalon? A fog bank rolls in often and cloaks the marshlands and surrounding areas until only the peak of Glastonbury Tor can be seen. In the 12th century, Gerald of Wales, a writer, alleged that he had discovered the tombs of Arthur and Gwenevere in 1191 atop the Tor. But the Tor is famous for something else: the Red Spring. And the descriptions of looking and feeling like blood? All true. This spring is a geological wonder and tied to Grail lore and Celtic mythology.

And, lastly, the Spear of Lleu that weeps blood is

a must in Grail lore. But more on this in book three's *Historical Notes*.

Well, now for the part I know you're all really waiting for.

Gwenevere.

Who was she really? As our story hints at, she's not some simpering fair maiden who is sold off for political alliances. My progressive, feminist sensibilities won't endlessly wax poetic the Gwenevere (or Guinevere) stuffed down our post-Victorian throats. Why? This barren, damsel-in-distress Queen isn't historical anyway, just part of the late Medieval, Victorian, and post-Victorian romance glamour that perfectly mirrored their ideal "Lady": gentle, fair, blonde, submissive to men, but who is easily led astray by her feeble, romantic heart. An "Eve" archetype character. So, ladies take note, do not end up like Gwenevere and become a homewrecker. Be a happy kept woman, instead.

Ick.

The *real* Gwenevere of legends is more powerful than Arthur and doesn't need a man. Rather, a man needs her to become king—which is Celtic pagan beliefs at its core. The woman is the life giver, the spring from which all creation and power stems. But first, we need to break down a few words.

"Gwen" is an old Cymry (Welsh) word for a young woman who was so profoundly beautiful that you would die if you gazed upon her for too long. It was a sacred or holy form of beauty tied to being a sun or moon demi-goddess, or perhaps even a goddess of light. When I look at the beauty of the sun directly, I want to die. I get it. *shrugs*

Gwenevere (Welsh: Gwenhwyfar) is a direct cognate of the Irish name Findabair (or Fionnabhair). Yup, the idea of a "Gwenevere" first came from 1ˢᵗ century Ireland and mentioned in *The Ulster Cycle* as the daughter of Queen Medb of Connacht, who later inspired Shakespeare's Queen Mab—a faerie queen. Findabair / Gwenhwyfar came from a line of earth-and-sovereignty goddesses—sídhe faeries who married a king to his land either through matrimony, sex, or the offering of sacred relics. A Celtic king was not truly king unless he was "sovereign blessed."

The first mention of a Gwenevere in Arthurian lore is Arthur's faerie bride. And, sadly, they weren't in love. In fact, Gwenhwyfar runs away and Arthur hunts her down and brings her back to his land, not because of love, but because he couldn't be King without her. The Celts believed that the land reflected the health of their King. If he were maimed, injured, or terminally ill, the people would demand a new king to ensure their land remained bountiful as his injury would demonstrate that he was clearly out of favor with the earth goddess who married him to the land.

Not a very romantic origin story for one of the most romanticized female characters and relationships in the history of literature. The irony is sadly delightful.

Historical inaccuracies: Medieval Inns weren't a thing until the 14ᵗʰ century. But, since this is also fantasy, we bent the timeline a bit to suit our storytelling needs.

Well, that's it for this segment. Stay tuned for book three, THE FIRST GWENEVERE, where I'll discuss the mythological origins of Morgana, Merlin, Galahad, Percival, and Lancelot, as well as share about the Four Ancient Artifacts of Ireland and how they inspired the Welsh Arthurian Legend tales.

All errors that may exist while trying to represent Celtic and Welsh culture, mythology, geography, and Arthurian Legend elements are entirely mine. I am a storyteller, weaving together information that builds and forms worlds in our imaginations. In the famous words of Nennius, a 9th century Celtic monk, "I have made a heap of all that I could find."

Your *Knights of Caerleon* lore keeper,

Jesikah Sundin

More Books

Claire Luana & Jesikah Sundin

THE KNIGHTS OF CAERLEON
The Fifth Knight, book 1
The Third Curse, book 2
The First Gwenevere, book 3

Claire Luana

MOONBURNER CYCLE
Moonburner, book 1
Sunburner, book 2
Starburner, book 3
Burning Fate, prequel

THE CONFECTIONER'S GUILD
The Confectioner's Guild, book 1
The Confectioner's Truth, book 2
The Confectioner's Coup, book 3
The Confectioner's Exile, prequel

Jesikah Sundin

THE BIODOME CHRONICLES
Legacy, book 1
Elements, book 2
Transitions: Novella Collection, book 2.5
Gamemaster, book 3

CLAIRE LUANA grew up reading everything she could get her hands on and writing every chance she could. Eventually, adulthood won out, and she turned her writing talents to more scholarly pursuits, going to work as a commercial litigation attorney.

While continuing to practice law, Claire decided to return to her roots and try her hand once again at creative writing. She has written and published the Moonburner Cycle and the forthcoming Confectioner Chronicles, a trilogy about magical food. She is currently working on the Knights of Caerleon trilogy, an Arthurian Legend fantasy romance series, which she is co-writing with Jesikah Sundin. She lives in Seattle, Washington with her husband and two dogs. In her (little) remaining spare time, she loves to hike, travel, binge-watch CW shows, and of course, fall into a good book.

www.claireluana.com

JESIKAH SUNDIN is a multi-award winning Ecopunk SciFi and Forest Fantasy writer mom of three nerdlets and devoted wife to a gamer geek. In addition to her family, she shares her home in Monroe, Washington with a red-footed tortoise and a collection of seatbelt purses. She is addicted to coffee, laughing, and Dr. Martens shoes ... Oh! And the forest is her happy place.

www.jesikahsundin.com
www.jesikahsundin.com/moontreebooks